THE MERCHANTS

Gerry Pratt

Copyright © 2013 Gerry Pratt

All rights reserved, including the right to reproduce this book or portions thereof in any form whatsoever

This is a work of fiction. Names, characters, places and incidents portrayed in this novel are either the product of the author imagination or are used fictitiously. Any resemblance to actual events or locals or persons, living or dead is entirely coincidental.

Cover Photo Library of Congress, Prints & Photographs Division, Detroit Publishing Company Collection, LC-DIG-ggbain-11656

DEDICATION

For Barbara June, the Knitress in my life.

And with special thanks to Barbara Blackhurst, my publisher, who worked so hard to bring this to print.

Other books by Gerry Pratt

God is Blue

Love Never Dies

In Search of a Hero

ACKNOWLEDGMENTS

Thanks to my editor Beatrice Halfner, her hard work, scrutiny and dedication have not gone unnoticed. Without her diligence these books would not have made it to print.

PROLOGUE

The seeds of Wolfe & Bloomberg were planted in the spring of 1887 by Asa Lutsk Wolfe, a thirty-year-old Austrian immigrant with funds entrusted to him by his extended family. By the year 1913, the business had blossomed into a family-run corporation occupying a block-square anchor store overlooking the waterfront on the corner of Hastings and Main. Asa's early hardware inventory of picks, shovels and saws, along with sacks of grain to serve early settlers, was supplanted over time with lines of fine furnishings, jewelry, china and high fashion men's and women's ready-to-wear. As the business grew into a three-state merchandising empire, it became the popular myth that no one could sell at a price lower than Asa Wolfe's 'Big Store'. Stories of Asa's merchandising genius grew each day of his life, becoming the mixed legacy for his only son to emulate, if he could.

Yet Isaiah Wolfe was about to lose it all, his heritage, the power passed into his hands to control the world of Wolfe & Bloomberg as his own. The extended family investors were already planning the move that would culminate in kicking him into the street. He knew how it would happen; it was his own formula for losers. First they would paint his name from the parking-lot curb, and as a final coup de feu fatal, send a maintenance man for his keys to the store. In time, even the family name would be erased from the store marquee, where the reputation, "never to be undersold," had served as an ambiguous claim for a century or more.

CHAPTER 1: A ROTTEN DAY TO SELL

An October wind muscled its way up Main Street, snapping the wet awnings over the street entrance to Wolfe & Bloomberg, the 'Big Store'. From his eighth- floor window, Isaiah's eyes were focused on the raindrops dribbling down the window glass. "A rotten day to sell," he shouted. "This damn weather is punching a helluva hole in the October numbers."

Isaiah was aware he was shouting at a window, but he was picturing the red face of Mike Prier, the overweight publisher of the city's two newspapers. He felt stronger and taller after shouting at the much larger publisher. It was an essential element in his bartering for rates the paper would charge volume advertisers.

"Besides, the bastard and his country club friends could go..." he left the thought unfinished, having never been certain of the Semitic prejudice he had in mind. "You suckered me into an eight-page special supplement, both papers at eleven hundred dollars a page," he continued to shout. "And there's not a damn customer in the store. We could have drawn a bigger crowd advertising a farting contest."

Isaiah puckered and pressed his lips against the window, his lip prints forming a cold, ephemeral valentine on the glass, a replica of the lipstick prints on love notes from his mother. He considered a running leap at the window that might carry him through the glass. The thought of his vertiginous fall was quickly followed by mind-pictures of his flying eight stories to the pavement. He could feel the raindrops striking his face, his coat tails flapping in the wind like broken wings as he fell. Flying past the ladies' third-floor ready-to-wear dressing rooms, he stared back at the startled women shielding their pubic hair from the eyes of a dying man.

Those rooms had been Isaiah's introduction to the big store. On the day of his first visit, he was squeezed into one of those dressing rooms with his mother while he watched – with questionable innocence – as she squeezed her naked rump into silk bloomers two or three sizes too small for her overweight body.

Isaiah knew all the floors. From his eighth floor office, his fall became an elevator ride. Radios. Televisions. Recordings. Hardware. Garden Tools. Going down. Home Furnishing. Men's Suits. Neckties and Shoes. Ladies Lingerie. Ready to wear. Main Floor. Candies. Cosmetics. Sundries. And Diamonds. (Isaiah himself had created a separate department for diamonds). Costume Jewelry. Splat. A shiver ran through his body as he pictured himself bouncing off the canvas awning, flipping high into the air and flopping into the curbside gutter, a lump of soggy flesh awash in the sewer-bound runoff.

But Isaiah's office window glass was laced with wire mesh. He couldn't jump through that glass even if he took a running leap. Besides, the years of repainting had sealed the sash, a comforting realization, releasing him from the terror of his imaginary fall. He shivered again and rubbed his sleeve on the glass attempting to erase his lip print. No point in leaving the lips of a dead man on the glass, though a farewell kiss did appeal to his morbid state of mind.

He looked out from his sanctuary from death, willing himself to die, all the while refusing to acknowledge the insistent voice from the intercom box on his desk demanding attention. He was a ghost, suffocating in a steam-heated office, an invisible spirit.

"Did you hear what I said? I'm going for coffee." The husky, female voice broadcast through the office with startling clarity. Isaiah glared at the varnished-oak speaker box.

"What in hell happened to my will?" he shouted at the box. "I'm a dying man. You said so yourself. When a man is about to die, he needs a will."

"Did you look in your basket?" the voice replied with condescending impatience.

Isaiah glanced down on the large blue legal folder. "And what happened to my call to George Black?"

"George Black?" The question asked with a note of uncertainty.

"Yes, George Black. Black, Higgins, Kennedy, Gardner and Black," he screamed. A muffled groan from the varnished box was followed by the sound of Lillian Zaronis punching out the number.

The intercom was a tool Isaiah installed when he first took over as chief executive of the big store, insuring his survival through the subsequent years of inter-family fratricide. A hidden switch concealed beneath his desk enabled him to listen in on any desk on the executive floor offices. He could do this by simply switching the speaker from office to office, desk to desk, without the others suspecting his ear was at their door.

Asa Wolfe, Isaiah's father, had preached an appreciation of cunning care of such issues. Isaiah had realized too late that the old man had taught others as well. Surveying the window once more he watched as his lips and the bulbous print of his nose began to reappear on the glass. Lillian Zaronis' voice summoned him from his fantasies.

"I have George Black on the line." The box heaved a sigh of exasperation.

"Please," Isaiah replied in mock submission. "Put him on."

"I'm going downstairs," she reminded him.

"Isaiah?" The voice of the most sophisticated and expensive law firm in the city leapt out of the box. Isaiah hesitated, waiting for the sound of his secretary hanging up the phone. "Isaiah? Hello? George Black here?" There followed an audible click.

"Black." Isaiah was incapable of conversational ceremonies. "I need a lawyer. Are you for hire?" He'd managed to make it sound as if he were hailing a taxi.

"Good morning, Isaiah. It's good to hear from you. And how are things at the store?" Black was dodging, already aware of the meaning behind this unusual call.

"God damn it, Black." Isaiah struggled to control his voice. "I need a lawyer." He could picture the grey haired, smooth-faced attorney smiling patiently at his display of impetuous temper. "Answer my God damn question."

"Isaiah. You wish to engage our firm? Is that what you are saying?"

There was only silence while Isaiah silently cursed the slick bastard on the other end of the call. He had offered him the job. What the hell was the necessity of his beating around the bush? Damn lawyers are expensive and they charge by the minute, running up their bills with telephone bullshit.

"Isaiah?" Black decided to quit playing games. "You know there is nothing we would like more than to represent you or the store. Just as you must be aware that I'm always here to help, in any way I can. What is it you have in mind?"

There was no response. Isaiah's sulking failed to irritate the lawyer, who surged on confidently. "You and I have known each other too long to bullshit one another, Isaiah. Frankly, my partners and I would have reservations in representing you or your organization in conjunction with your present counsel."

"You mean you won't work with that sonovabitch Rosenthal? Well, he's out. I don't have a lawyer. Not a single, God damn lawyer. Does that satisfy you?" Black could hear the sound of Isaiah's voice beginning to crack.

"Let me get this straight, Isaiah. You are saying that Abe Rosenthal is no longer representing you or the firm?" Black's voice softened. "I don't understand." The lawyer was stalling, adjusting his approach, aware that Isaiah Wolfe wouldn't so much as go to the toilet without being certain the psychopath Rosenthal was nowhere in the store. Still, there was only silence from Isaiah's end of the call.

"Isaiah, you know we are always ready to serve you and your family. You will recall we represented Rosa's interest in the settlement of her father's estate." Black was purposefully reviving Isaiah's memory of what he and the eighty-six lawyers who attached their names to his had done in carving up Rosa Wolfe's inheritance. "Exactly what do you have in mind, Isaiah?"

Black was approaching Isaiah Wolfe as he would an unfriendly witness, cautiously establishing the territory he was prepared to discuss in a telephone conversation. Black was aware that there was trouble at the big store. What little stock that was traded publicly had been all but dormant until recently. It was now moving up in volume. The attorney's thinking began to adjust closer to the heart of what he sensed was coming.

"You should know, our firm has picked up a little of the troubles at Wolfe & Bloomberg. It has come to us in bits and pieces. However I don't suppose it would hurt to share a few of the details that have reached us.

"I recently received a call from a New York Investment Bank representing Regal Partners," the attorney explained, followed by a seconds-long silence while he paused for a possible rebuttal.

"Regal Partners is one of the largest leverage-buyout firms in the country, Isaiah. I am allowed to share this with you only because we have turned down the opportunity to represent the bank's interest. However, our contact with the bank revealed that Regal has been in discussions with the Bloomberg family. To put it candidly, the bank is confident of Regal's plans to acquire your company.

"My partners and I believe there have been too many local concerns selling out to out-of-state corporations. That kind of ownership is not good for our firm, nor is it good for anyone making a living in this state.

"However, the bank convinced us that Regal Partners has the Bloomberg family committed to their acquisition. If that's indeed the case, you can be reasonably sure the bank has done the homework. With the financing on board, the consensus in our office is that they might well pull off the deal.

"Isaiah, I'm sorry you waited this long to call. If what I now believe has happened, you will at least know how our firm feels about this trend to outside ownership."

Black heaved a long, theatrical sigh intended for the little man's ears. "Unfortunately, Isaiah, I'm going to be in depositions through the afternoon. However, I could have Patrick Higgins come over and talk. That would help give us a leg up on where things stand before you decide that you want us to become involved. Would that help?"

"No. Goddamit. That won't. I don't need to talk and I don't want your flunkies." Isaiah's voice broke in what sounded like a sob on the attorney's end of the telephone.

"Can't you understand? My life is coming apart. These aren't cigar store Indians about to roast me alive that you can buy off with a few beads and a line of legal bullshit. These are black-hearted, vengeful bastards who are about to throw my ass out into the street."

Isaiah Wolfe's pleading was out of character, his candor momentarily confusing the lawyer. Black knew the little merchandising legend by his reputation as a tyrannical, posturing, demanding, self-important, insecure ego. The attorney, who was seldom at a loss for words, was dumbfounded.

"And I guess you know who I have to thank for this?" Isaiah added bitterly. "Your old law school pal, Abraham Rosenthal."

It was true. Black and Abe Rosenthal had graduated from Harvard Law School in the same year. Black played on the Harvard football team while Rosenthal beat him out for a voice on the Harvard Law Review. Their competitive differences had transcended to bitterness ever since. Recently, Black declined appointment to the State Supreme Court, choosing to remain in private practice with the firm bearing his name that was founded by his father. The court appointment Black declined was an honor Rosenthal coveted and for which he was never considered.

"Well, that does it," Black sighed. "If Rosenthal is on the other side in this fight, I'll have to take a hand. We can have another lawyer from the firm handle the depositions. You have my attention, Isaiah. I'll be in your office within the hour," Black replied quietly.

Isaiah's temperament, his solipsistic manner of showing disdain and absolute authority over whomever he dealt with, had his hand in motion to slam down the receiver without exchanging another word. Only the uncertainty of the moment delayed him long enough to hear that Black was not finished talking.

"We will need you to gather up a set of bylaws, Isaiah. And we need the minutes from the past three or four board meetings. You do have board meetings?" Black asked doubtfully.

Again, there was no answer.

"Regardless, we will need the articles of incorporation; plus any agreements between you and the Bloomberg heirs, proxies, stockholders lists, everything you have. Isaiah, I know you are reluctant to discuss the details of the company business, but this is not the time to play your cards close to the vest. We are starting from scratch and we are going to need everything pertaining to the corporate structure. Have it ready. And Isaiah, I'm going to be asking Patrick Higgins along to sit in."

"Black," Isaiah wailed. "I have already tried kissing Jake's ass. It won't work."

"Jake? Jacob Bloomberg?"

"Jake is the one making all the family decisions now," Isaiah replied.

George Black was unable to disguise his gasp of incredulity. Isaiah's second cousin, Jacob Bloomberg, was the corporate cripple, and had been for the much of his entire twenty-eight years. Jake survived in the firm because of the family name on the marquee and the income from his father Nathan's stock held in the Bloomberg family trust.

However, there were a number of shares of Bloomberg stock that remained in the hands of distant cousins. Most of that stock was voted by Isaiah, as it was by his father. The agreement was extended to the son in a non-documented agreement with the elder

Bloomberg the year Isaiah rescued him from a political scandal during Nathan's campaigning for senator.

Isaiah set the phone in its cradle without saying anything further. He was too exhausted to go on talking. He went to the window once more, watching the raindrops slide down the glass.

The customers? What would they care if he jumped? He pictured looking up into the faces of the crowd stretching over the shoulders of the police for a closer look. 'Hey. Hey. That's Isaiah Wolfe lying on the curb. Ugly little putz. Looks worse with his neck broken.' He could hear them, hovering over his broken body; faces that owed the store money. He had seen enough of them in the credit department, wringing their hands with their lies, wearing clothes stolen from ready-to-wear, their bellies filled with the lunch from the store dining room, where they had walked out without paying. Lunch on Isaiah Wolfe? Why not? He's dead.

CHAPTER 2: ENTER GEORGE BLACK

The lawyer paused at the threshold to Isaiah's office, pausing long enough for Isaiah to look up and see him framed in the dark-stained oak doorway. George Black was a glowing portrait of himself, even without the oak frame. Six feet and handsome, in a stylishly cut, double breasted suit, carefully set tie, and manicured nails, he looked like a fashion model from Men's Suits on the third floor. The image was betrayed by his reputation for a shrewd legal mind and a courtroom manner that could be gentle and kind one minute and devastatingly cruel the next. Isaiah ignored the professional smile and Black's outstretched hand and appeared to turn away.

"All that good-will bullshit going to be tacked on to my fee, Black?" Isaiah muttered.

Black dropped his outstretched hand without losing his smile as Isaiah wheeled, his tiny hands darting out to seize the lapels of the lawyer's suit. With a quick twist of the wrist he exposed the label inside the jacket and sneered.

"Brioni. Handmade. Italian. How much? A thousand? Two? Three grand? What's the matter, Black? What are we doing wrong? Our suits not good enough for you? You can't wear a Hickey Freeman? Louis Roth? Oxford? You have to go to New York and take the bread from out of my mouth?" Isaiah turned away before Black could answer.

"Look this over." he snapped, tossing the blue legal folder to the lawyer. "Somewhere in all that bullshit Abe Rosenthal names himself my trustee and executor. I want you to change that right now. I could be dead any minute. I could be starving to death with people like you taking your business to New York," he snapped.

Black dropped into an empty chair, smoothed the lapels on his suit and opened the folder.

"Slow down, Isaiah. You are all steamed up. You are not dead and I doubt very much that my suit is going to put a dint in your sales."

"You came up from the main floor. You saw it yourself. We are paying for an eight-page ad, a thousand dollars a page special section, all editions. God only knows what we spent on radio. From sundries to men's shirts, the store is so quiet on the main floor; you could hear a canary fart. Don't tell me we don't need your business. How in hell am I supposed to pay you? Eh? Answer me that."

Isaiah plopped onto his throne, a high-backed, padded chair behind the desk. He spun the chair so that the tall back was to the lawyer. It was a practiced gesture, completely hiding his diminutive body so that anyone on the other side of the desk was left facing what appeared to be an empty desk.

The attorney began leafing through the documents, muttering page by page. "This entire instrument is structured around Abe Rosenthal and his firm as trustee and executors. His discretionary powers pertain to every disposition. Isaiah, unless you want your estate tied up in a legal mess for years, we must take the time to revise this document with care. Besides, much of it is outdated. How long ago did you write this?"

Before Isaiah could answer, the middle-aged, rumpled body of Lillian Zaronis appeared in the doorway followed by a man whose thinning, black hair was carefully combed across his forehead so that it looked like a religious cowl. Pat Higgins, six-foot four or more, towered over the stodgy secretary, his muscular sloping shoulders filling the entire doorway.

"Ah. Patrick's here." Black got to his feet. "Isaiah, you have never met Pat Higgins from our office. Pat heads up our litigation team. Pat, you know who Isaiah Wolfe is, of course."

Isaiah spun his chair to face the visitor, audibly muttering his appraisal while eyeing Higgins. "Black Irish. The worst kind.

Drink like hell. Will screw anything that doesn't bite. Know anything about wills, Higgins? Or are you just the firm's bullshit artist?" Isaiah was establishing turf. "George," he snapped without waiting for a response from Higgins' bemused grin. "Let the man see that will of mine."

"What I know about estate law, Mister Wolfe, George Black could fit into a single page of his day calendar and still have the page mostly blank." Higgins smiled. "I follow George around merely for the chance to read his briefs." Isaiah felt his edge fading as he watched the two lawyers close ranks. George Black went on as if nothing had been said.

"Isaiah, this business is much too serious for you and me to go on fooling with one another in this fashion. I can understand you being upset with Rosenthal, but there are ethical considerations that —"

"God damn it, whose side are you on?" Isaiah shouted. Under normal circumstances, Black's mentioning 'ethical considerations' would have led him to suspect a lawyer-to-lawyer conspiracy with Rosenthal. But knowing what he did about Black and Rosenthal, he was certain there could be no liaison, no matter what the game, nor the stakes. Treachery had been lost on the chairman and chief executive of Wolfe & Bloomberg, honing Isaiah's paranoia to a destructive edge. But the well-publicized history of the bitter animosity between Black and Rosenthal, some of which had involved a Bar Association reprimand, eliminated the possibilities of a conspiracy. Lawyer-to-lawyer legal intrigue was not one of Isaiah's worries.

"Isaiah, drawing a new will for an estate the size of yours involves many considerations. There are serious distribution matters, trusts and taxes and —"

Isaiah cut him off. "What do you take me for? A kike? You have me mixed up with Rosenthal. I told you. The estate is yours. You take care of the details."

"Especially," Black continued, ignoring the interruption," if you intend to name our firm to replace Abe Rosenthal as administrator-trustee." He handed the will to the younger lawyer. "If it makes you feel any better, Isaiah, Patrick can invalidate this document before we leave this afternoon. But you are going to have to spend time with our office on a new will and trust document, immediately. We will schedule a meeting with your accountants and our tax people later. Abe Rosenthal never has claimed to be much of an estate tax attorney anyway."

The lawyer paused, searching for signs of agreement in Isaiah Wolfe's angry frown. Turning to Higgins, he added, "Pat, let's get this taken care of before we go any farther so we can get down to the issues facing the company. Isaiah, will you call your secretary in here? She is, I believe, also a notary?"

Isaiah muttered an order into the communication box and Lillian reappeared, her usual, disheveled figure slouching with exaggerated disinterest. Curiosity appeared to have forced her to miss her coffee break, though she was making no effort to disguise her practiced look of indifference. Higgins, having heard rumors of the battles between Isaiah Wolfe and his secretary, couldn't check the question posed by his imagination. 'How in hell did he ever put up with this babe for one minute?'

"Would you bring in your pad, Miss," Higgins said.

The secretary cast a questioning glance across the room to Isaiah for confirmation.

"Please," George Black said coldly. "We are pressed for time, Miss Zaronis." She went back to her desk, retrieved her dictation book, and took the chair beside Isaiah's desk.

Higgins spent the next ten minutes dictating a brief over-riding codicil. Then, almost as an afterthought, he turned to Isaiah. "I'm sure you have thoughts on who you want as your new trustees? Someone you would be comfortable with until we get a more permanent document?"

There was no response, only a moment of indecision reflected in Isaiah's frown.

"Perhaps George Black and your friend?" The enquiry hung uncomfortably in the sudden silence. Isaiah glared at Higgins, uncertain whether the young lawyer had uttered a brazenly cheeky suggestion or had spoken in keen candor, an element he knew he urgently needed.

"Name her, but don't tell her," he snapped. "And if you need a third, ask Paul Gold," he added dryly. Higgins didn't wait for an explanation but went on dictating to the secretary, naming Desdemona Patricia Gonne trustee.

"Desdemona? That sounds like somebody Othello murdered," muttered George Black. "Who is this Desdemona Patricia Gonne?"

Neither Isaiah nor Higgins answered.

"Isaiah? Patrick? This Desdemona? Who is this person?" Black demanded.

"What difference does it make, who she is?" Isaiah said defiantly. "Ask your young expert here. He's the one poking his nose into other people's business. She's my executor. Doesn't that make her something?"

"It certainly does," Black muttered, deciding to let the matter rest, for now.

Patrick, turning to Lillian, smiled with a trace of condescension. "Going through this document, it appears that your name appears among the beneficiaries, Miss Zaronis. All we have changed in the codicil is the naming of the trustees. However, that means you won't do as a witness to the new document, nor as the notary," he added. "In the event this document listing you as the notary were to be challenged, that would have presented a problem. Meantime, honey..."

"Honey my ass," Lillian muttered, rising from her chair.

"That may well be the place for it," Higgins continued nonplussed. "However, would you please call our office and have one of our notaries join Mr. Black and me with her book to witness Mister Wolfe's signature?"

"Pay no attention to her," Isaiah added quickly. "She's been infected with visions of grandeur. Go ahead and tell him," he said, indicating Higgins. "Tell him you are planning on leaving me high and dry for an ephemeral career in politics. She's running for city commissioner," he said, as if the idea bored him.

Lillian was already headed for the office doorway, muttering deprecating curses for having been addressed as honey. "Next thing you know, she'll be running for mayor," Isaiah shouted after her, tugging nervously at his heavy black eyebrows. "God only knows what that would do to this city."

"You need a witness?" Isaiah muttered. "What the hell. Call someone in from the outer office." He paused, thinking better of the suggestion, adding quietly. "Better ask if they would mind."

"It's not merely a witness. We need a notary who is not mentioned as a beneficiary. Miss Zaronis should never have signed the original document as the notary," Higgins said, with a trace of impatience. He rose to call out to the outer office where Lillian was still talking to herself.

"Miss Zaronis, we will need three copies." The secretary refused to answer.

"Mister Wolfe," Higgins continued, "what we are completing is a temporary document. It may give you some personal comfort, but we need to get on with something that will stand a much better chance in a contested probate. I suggest we take a look at the documents George asked you to have ready for us," he added.

"Isaiah, why don't you back up and tell us what you meant by Jake Bloomberg making all the decisions for Wolfe & Bloomberg," Black said. "If we are going to help, Pat and I need a handle on what's going on here and who the players are."

"I'm still running the corporation," Isaiah answered. "What I said was Jake is making all the decisions for the Bloomberg family. And somehow he has gotten his hands on the list of the Bloomberg cousins who have granted me their proxies. Without those proxies, cousin Jake is going to run me out of here."

CHAPTER 3: ROSA LINTEL

Sam and Esther Lintel, along with their teenaged daughter Rosa, owned and operated the New York millinery broker Lintel & Associates. Rosa first came face to face with Asa Wolfe during his annual buying trip to New York. She overheard his cussing long before she ever saw him while he went storming through her family's warehouse, deprecating everything he saw at the top of his lungs.

"This merchandise was old a year ago," Asa growled. "The hats you are showing me are nothing but dreck." He was using the Yiddish term for shit to drive his message home. "You expect me to be wasting three hundred dollars' expense, traveling three days on a train, to buy last year's hats? You think I'm coming all the way to New York to buy yesterday's hats? For you to rob me?"

Sam Lintel continued assuring him. "These are all the latest New York styles. You see these hats on Broadway; you see them in the good salons. I promise you."

Asa continued turning his back on everything Sam showed him, until the moment he discovered Rosa. She had suddenly appeared as if magically summoned from out of nowhere. She was tall and full-breasted, high in the hips like a fine Morgan saddle-bred mare, with the purple-tinged, brown eyes of a colt. Asa was close to forty, with short, wiry hair, and a dry, burning passion on his lips that seemed forever on fire with the biting sarcasm that continually soured his entire face.

Asa would swear until the day he died, the moment Rosa appeared in the doorway to her father's office, he heard celestial music. During that first meeting, he would confess in years to come, a weakness took possession of his limbs, until he feared his knees were knocking so hard the sound could be heard throughout the room. Displaying considerable chutzpah, even for Asa who was never considered shy, he went to her and took her hands in his.

"And who are you?" he asked in subdued astonishment.

"Rosa Lintel," she replied, attempting to pull her hands free of his hot fingers, the chill in her voice revealing her indignation at Asa's criticism of her father's merchandise. Asa refused to release her hand. "This is my family's business, Mister Wolfe," she added, making it perfectly clear she had overheard his berating the millinery from which he had come to buy.

"You know my name," Asa smiled. "That's good. Do you know where I come from?"

"Yes, I do." Even as a virgin Rosa was saying something to him with her eyes that any man could understand. Asa openly marveled at what he beheld. She read his thoughts. "I am sixteen," she said in obvious rebuke, with a mere hint of promise.

"I see. I see. Sometime perhaps you will come out west and visit us. We have a big country for big women like you. You would be the beauty, the great beauty of the West."

"Thank you, I'm sure," she replied coldly.

Eighteen months and two buying trips later, following his sleepless dreams of the teen-aged New York beauty, Asa proposed to her father that he allow Rosa to visit the West.

"My own mother will be her chaperone," Asa promised. "What's there to worry about? Keep her in New York and she meets one of these fast-talking Irish-New York shegetz fresh off the boat. Then what do you have on your hands? Trouble. Send her west, Sam. Every girl needs a vacation, Sam. We can find her a mishpocha, for a really good, suitable marriage. Nothing without your approval, Sam. My mother would see to that."

Sam Lintel nodded knowingly without comment, indicating he would consider the suggestion. It required the passing of another year before Sam agreed, and the nineteen-year-old, soon to be twenty, Rosa Lintel, travelling alone in a private compartment, rode the Union Pacific Trans Continental west. She never returned to New York until much later in life, but within a month wrote to her parents asking for their permission to be engaged to be married to the proprietor of one of the largest department stores west of the Mississippi River. That was the boast of Wolfe & Bloomberg, based on the square block emporium swallowing up every inch of ground from Hastings Street to the waterfront.

However, it was merely an engagement. Rosa put off agreeing to marry Asa for over ten years, despite the fact that within a year of arriving in the West, she was pregnant with Asa's stillborn son. Isaiah, born eighteen months later, was to be her second and only child.

The engagement and the pregnancies were as much the result of Rosa's own intensive planning and Momma Lintel's instructions as they were due to the lust in Asa's loins. There was very little about men, young or old, large or small, Rosa did not understand. But Asa was a preoccupied man, and having read somewhere that a man dissipates his creative powers when over indulging in sex, purposefully avoided the needs of his sloe-eyed young bride as often as his lust could be held in check. Instead, Asa turned his creative powers into twelve and often sixteen-hour days in the store.

Dispassionately and at first discreetly, Rosa learned to look elsewhere. One of those who sought eagerly to fulfill her needs was Asa's cousin, Nathan Bloomberg. Nathan and the scattered Bloomberg stockholders were the owners of the controlling shares of Wolfe & Bloomberg, much of which was purchased when cash was king during the crash of 1903. Ever since, Nate was constantly on the alert for picking up whatever else he could that belonged to Asa; especially his generously endowed, dark-eyed young wife.

He made it his business to keep informed of Rosa's nocturnal and mid-afternoon forays into the ranks of store drivers and clerks. The knowledge that lesser men were being accepted drove him to constant fawning, presents of anonymous gifts of jewelry and flowers, some which Rosa accepted. Nathan propositioned her with open proposals and once, in the garden of Asa's home, tried to take her with masculine authority, convinced that once she had tasted his love making, she would be his forever. Wrestling her to the lawn, he found himself sprawled in a bed of roses with a painful dislocation in his spine, and the sudden, frightening awareness of the strength of those feminine limbs he so ardently desired.

Forced to turn his passions to the legions of shop girls and secretaries, Nathan returned to his practice of finding romance through promises of promotions and personal favors.

CHAPTER 4: THE WEDDING

Isaiah Wolfe's introduction to the big store came the afternoon of August 18, 1913, three-months to the day before his tenth birthday. It was the week after his mother's finally agreeing she was prepared to marry Asa Wolfe, in the Temple before the rabbi, with their son a prominent guest. Rosa informed the welcoming committee gathered to receive her at the store that she and her son had come to buy a new wedding suit for Isaiah and a few things for herself.

Isaiah's only memory of his initial visit to Wolfe & Bloomberg was of being squeezed into the crowded dressing cubicle and watching – with questionable innocence – his Mother peel off her satin corsets to force her wattle arms and bosoms into one dress after another. In that dressing room, enveloped in body odors and perfume, forced to breathe the stifling air and the confining heat of the crowded room, Isaiah planted his first kiss on the mirrored wall, leaving the traces of his lips imprisoned on the glass. Kissing the glass that day made the first impression in the boy's mind, that the cool kiss was an avenue of escape from the cluttered confines of the dressing room. It became his means of escaping reality, a means of extracting himself from any and all kinds of confrontations. It would stay with him through a lifetime.

The days leading up to and following the wedding were packed with opulent recognition of the place and power of Wolfe & Bloomberg. Isaiah's memories of those halcyon parties were retained in mind pictures of Japanese paper lanterns, pink and blue and orange, strings of them swaying in the evening breeze. Their tiny candles casting a mysterious light over the swimming pool. There was fresh lemonade that gave Isaiah a belly ache and diarrhea for two days, along with the smoke of kosher wieners cooking on an open grill with toasted buns. And there were the strangers, crowds of them recruited to bring a festive feeling to the celebration, wolfing down the wieners and toasted buns and beer. Without so much as a glance at the Japanese lanterns casting colored shadows over the pool.

Rosa made her appearance at the reception crowned with a hat created especially by her father, with feathers and bows that would have moved the S.S. Lusitania in a soft breeze. She was photographed surrounded by the smiling faces of young party guests, faces Isaiah came to recognize behind the cosmetics counter or standing diffidently in store smocks, clerking in housewears. As for ten-year-old Isaiah, fitted in his new plus fours and deep-blue tweeds, Rosa proclaimed he could have been mistaken for the Duke of Windsor, except for his having inherited Asa's nose. It was an image that became a part of how Isaiah saw himself, until his fateful years in an Austrian boys' school. Though in that year, the year of his mother's wedding, the Duke was already ten years older than Isaiah.

Isaiah learned to know the store in the shadow of his mother, the linens and silks, the feminine smells pervading most everything that lay beyond the large brass-trimmed doors. He also began to understand the diffidence Rosa Wolfe received whenever she passed by, especially from the male clerks, in their tight-fitting dark suits with their smiles supported by debonair mustaches or mutton chop sideburns and celluloid collars. Rosa was the wife of the founder, and there were rumors in the store about that large Jewish bosom and the sensuous full lips every man in the store knew were not properly being cared for, at least, not by an aging and preoccupied Asa Wolfe.

CHAPTER 5: ASA'S SELLING TECHNIQUES

They could have charged admission to Wolfe & Bloomberg following the installation of the first elevators to come to the city. Crowds came merely to ride the brass cages, the new magic lifts carrying customers from the main floor up and down six stories. A white-gloved starter would click her signal to the elevator operator to slide shut the folding doors as the rattling cages lurched loose from the main floor. With the elevator groaning in uncertain lunges and lifts, and the passenger's stomachs slipping sickeningly between their knees, the operator would call out the passing floors. "Lingerie, millinery, linens, ladies' ready-to-wear, second floor."

First-time riders would grow silent in apprehension watching the operator juggle the controls to bring the cage into proximity with each floor. A ride in the elevator became the crowning moment for a day at the big store. The escalators came later under Isaiah's direction, with the addition of the top three floors.

Isaiah's father's office was on the sixth floor, a modest room left vacant through the day while Asa Wolfe prowled the building, like a whiskered demon, in search of customers "doing business."

Isaiah recalled his father once scolding a persistent accounting clerk who cornered him to discuss the store's shrinking margins following a big sale. Asa pretended to believe that almost anything to do with balance sheets, operating statements and the company real estate was 'dreck.' "I'm just a poor peddler," he would snap at those who pressed him for administrative decisions. "What do you expect me to know about these things?"

"You expect me to understand your damn numbers?" he shouted at the accounting clerk. "All I need to know is that without customers, we are nothing but a warehouse. Don't come to me talking about profits and margin. You think my wife can wear all the dresses? You think we are saving the goods for a rainy day? We are peddlers. That's our business."

Asa Wolfe repeated this mantra through the store for thirty-five years; words that were to be echoed twenty years later in Isaiah's high-pitched, intense voice.

When sales were slow in a department like yard goods, Asa would come charging through the main aisle tumbling bundles of fabric from the shelves into heaps of gingham and towels on the floor. "There. Those are damaged goods." He would shout with wild satisfaction before stunned customers and clerks alike. "Take it all down to the basement. Put it on sale. We will call it our Bargain Basement sale. Half price. Everything damaged is half price. We don't have time for distressed merchandise. Sell it. If we keep it on the shelf another day it will begin to rot. If it rots it stinks. So sell it." And he would be gone, leaving havoc and sales in his wake.

Department managers, attempting to deflect his charge, would inevitably surrender, backing away with outstretched arms hoping to preserve what they could of their pristine displays. When Asa appeared, he would overturn anything moveable, knocking items from shelves, tearing apart or knocking over carefully constructed displays.

"A short customer can't reach these goods. Are we selling step ladders?" he would shout. "That's upstairs in hard goods. These sheets are piled too high for a short woman to touch and if she can't touch the fabric, she won't buy." And he would begin tearing down shelves and displays, rearranging the merchandise to look as if it had been handled. When he had the goods rearranged to his satisfaction, it didn't matter if it was clothing or yard goods, canned goods or hardware, he would take his marking pen and began slashing prices. That's when someone, usually one of the Bloomberg cousins, would slip away in search of Nathan.

With Nathan's arrival, the two sides would launch into battle, like opposing scrums in a rugby match, pushing back and forth in whichever department was under Asa's attack.

"You are acting like a herd of baboons. You don't know one end of this business from the other," Asa would shout at the clerks and cousin Nathan or anyone daring to question his price cutting. "As long as I'm running this business, keep your noses off the sales floor."

To which Nathan would shout back. "We know enough to know we cannot stay in business selling goods for less than we paid for them."

"Less than they cost us," his son Jake would echo meekly, only to bring a sharp, "Shut your mouth," from his father.

The Bloombergs were no match for Asa when the confrontation came to shouting, despite the fact there was some doubt as to who would run the business if it ever came to the point of the Bloombergs challenging Asa for control. Many of the Bloomberg relatives had become substantial stockholders in Wolfe & Bloomberg, as well as officers of the firm. Cousins, uncles, sons and nephews had all picked up or inherited stock over the years, and while Asa voted most of their proxies, there were no long-term agreements. But then that's the way Asa wanted things: both the battles on the main floor with the Bloombergs, and the uncertainty over whose responsibility it was to keep the place in business.

Those who knew him best were certain Asa lingered off the main floor with an eye constantly on the lookout for the elder Bloomberg. He was also rumored to possess the uncanny ability to anticipate the exact moment his overweight cousin would come charging down the stairs. Nathan seldom waited for the elevators when news of Asa's rampages reached him; he arrived with full-faced, fuzzy-cheeked son Jacob at his heel. Asa would meet the pair head on in the center of whatever department of the store he had been 'reorganizing, Asa's term for the chaos he created. Instantly, crowds of shoppers would be surrounding them like farmers at a cockfight.

Keeping a constant corner of his eye on the customers, Asa

would stand jowl to jowl with Nathan, until at the height of their shouting he would whip out a grease pencil and begin slashing the prices he had already slashed, accompanied by the wailing of the Bloomberg team.

"You have lost your mind. Somebody stop him. He's ruining us," Bloomberg would cry in anguish. "Lunatic. Stop."

Asa, feeding on his cousin's pain, would take that as a signal to increase his attack on the listed prices, the buying taking on a frenzied crush with customers fighting and pushing to get their hands on the goods. The arguments and shouting never ended, becoming merely an extension of the panic buying until the shelves were bare. By that point, the Bloombergs and Asa had abandoned their quarrel, joining every able body on the floor in sacking, wrapping, and moving out the goods marked to seemingly suicidal prices.

The customers were the last to realize, and very few ever did, that Asa had more often than not singled out large-margin items. Some staff members claimed he even came through the store in the evenings before a tirade to mark up prices in anticipation of his following day's attack on the department. If that were true, Asa never bothered to explain to the Bloombergs; he was certain he could never convince them to participate in his main-floor theatrics without their being convinced he was giving away the shirts off their backs.

Neither Nathan Bloomberg nor his son Jake could hold a candle to Asa when it came to merchandising. They were store executives and the main purpose of their existence, in Asa' Wolfe's mind, was to serve as straight men when sales were soft.

In his man-to-man conversations with seven-year-old Isaiah, Asa would explain. "My cousin Nathan's major value is that Nate is easier for me to handle than a baboon would be, and cousin Nate never shits on the floor."

"It is all about volume, son," he would whisper secretly into his son's ear during these conversations with the boy at his knee. "If you have the volume, there's no business for somebody else to open a store down the street. Don't worry about margin or making money on a sale. Get the customer. You are in business, so long as you have the customers. When we have no people in the stores, we are nothing. Do the business and making money will take care of itself."

For the secretive Asa Wolfe, the boy on his knee became a ventriloquist's doll, his large, dark eyes mesmerized by the deluge of words pouring over him on the stale breath of his father.

"One day we will do all the business, my son. All the business, and then even cousin Nathan won't worry about margin." He would laugh and squeeze Isaiah on his lap until the child's face showed the fear and discomfort at Asa's hugging.

That was the image Isaiah remembered when he took over the store, the image he attempted to emulate. The half-loved, half-feared, half-crazy old peddler left little room in his creation of Isaiah, his merchant prince, for the gentle, romantic soul nurtured in the fat, tender hands of his mother. Asa never dreamed or suspected what went on behind those large, soft eyes of his son; the secret, sensuous eyes that Asa mistook for the eyes of love.

CHAPTER 6: DESDEMONA GONNE

The parish church stood on Seventh or Eighth Avenue. It was so long ago, what with the factories and the small office buildings that have been erected where the school once stood, it is difficult to be certain of the church's location. But to those who remembered, it was a red brick edifice set back from a carpet of very green grass tended carefully by old-country Catholics. The stone steps leading to the heavy Spanish doors rose steeply from the sidewalk, up which the older nuns puffed and grunted on their way to attend morning Mass. The church rose solidly behind heavy Gothic doors with a steeple containing the Christ Jesus frozen in alabaster and concrete above the doors.

The nuns all lived in two thin, virginal houses that stood next to the church. Each morning before school they would file out of the residence, up the stone steps and into the church for pre-breakfast Mass. The candles, breathing a flickering light through the traces of incense, created a visible shroud over the tabernacle where their Jesus was waiting and watching for them from behind the small golden door.

When Father Frank Solinka arrived from the Quebec Catholic seminary, a twenty-eight-year-old farm-bred Saskatchewan boy, his head was filled with the world-saving burdens of having been selected to tend the souls of Our Lady of Perpetual Help Parish. He wore a flowing black soutane over his trousers and moved across the school yard with the eagerness of a Prairie farm boy discovering the city. His face reflected the ruddy traces of the prairie wind and the day-long sun of the farm. His hands and arms bore the heavy muscles and tendons of field work that would be with him until the day he died. When he laughed, his laughter would carry across the school grounds, and when he put his black boot to the school's soccer ball, it flew through the air so that you would think it had been fired from a gun.

It is easy now to see how Desdemona Patricia Gonne believed Father Frank Solinka would someday become a bishop, perhaps a cardinal. The sisters often complained there were none from Western Canada. In the recesses of Desdemona's imagination, where she spoke directly to God Himself, there were moments when the young priest appeared to her in the beehive crown and vestments worn by the thin-faced pontiff whose portrait hung in the school foyer.

"The trouble with you, Dessie Gonne, is you don't spend enough time on your Catechism. If you did, you would be out of here by three thirty with the rest of the class and I wouldn't have to waste my time watching you do what you should have done at home."

Sister Francis Clare was talking with her back to Dessie while working the blackboard brush over the chalk numbers from her recently dismissed arithmetic class. She stopped and cocked her head, her attention caught by the big flat voice of Father Solinka coming from somewhere in the vicinity of the gymnasium. He was singing.

"It's him again," the nun said irritably. "It's too bad that one didn't become a Trappist. He could sing all night to the glory of God with the monks, though he might find their vow of silence something of a hindrance. We would all be better off if he had a little less to say," the nun sighed. "But that'll be enough for today, Dessie. Get on with you before Father Solinka finds you here and wants to know why your Catechism wasn't finished."

Eagerly, the girl snatched up her books and with an over-the-shoulder "thank you" to the nun, began running from the classroom, drawn to the distant sounds of a street fair echoing across the bay.

Dessie Gonne was thirteen years old and looked much younger, the seat of her uniform worn and shining, her scuffed shoes turned in at the toes as she hurried out the door, intentionally slipping past the wide open gymnasium doors. She was dodging Father Solinka, who was busily occupied shooting a basketball at the gymnasium hoop. It was the last day of September and the final day of the street fair. Dessie, hearing the call of the calliope carrying across the waterfront, was unable to concentrate on the Blessed Virgin or anything but the music.

So she ran to the music, a child running to the lure of a calliope and a street fair and the promise of a good time. The afternoon sun felt hot on her shoulders through the coarse school uniform jersey, but the music was drawing ever nearer as she ran.

On reaching the fair she was disappointed to discover the grounds had been all but emptied of the noon-day crowds. The steam calliope had shut down for the afternoon; the music was originating from a speaker and a scratchy recording. All that remained of the exciting fair crowd were a handful of mothers, busily boxing ears and hollering at irascible children. The only sense of what the fair had once been was a lingering pollution of burning onions and fried food. The under-foot mess left by the week-long fair crowds, rising in the dusty, sun-dried air, added to the desolation. Even the megaphone shouting from the sideshow barkers had lost the enchantment of a Fair, blending into the cacophony of the late afternoon bustle of the city.

Dessie stopped to watch the huge Ferris wheel turning in circles in the sky, the empty seats rocking crazily as they tilted and rolled with each turn.

"You want to ride?" The heavy jowled Ferris wheel jockey asked, biting his lower lip as if he had just made a dubious decision.

Dessie shook her head, not to say 'no' emphatically, but in a way that said 'not really. It was an answer the wheel jockey read as 'I don't have any money.'

"I'll make you a deal." The wheel jockey seemed to roll rather than walk as he moved toward her, his thick fingers working over a handful of ticket stubs. The curiosity in her eyes gave way to an instant of wariness. "There's nothing to be afraid of," the man said. "You ride for nothing, but only if you holler."

"Holler?"

"When I get you up to the top, you start hollering like you are having the time of your life. Make it good and loud so people can hear you all over the park." He stopped the wheel, the empty seats rocking temptingly.

"Okay." Dessie jumped into the empty seat and the wheel jockey slapped the safety bar in place, winked and touched her on the knee.

"Good and loud now. I want everyone to hear how exciting it is up there. Make it good, and you can ride the rest of the afternoon." She nodded over the barking of the engine as the seat began to rise toward the sky.

A small circle gathered at the wheel, their expectant faces hovering over half-empty snow-cone shells as the girl rose above them into the fresh breeze coming up off the bay. She threw her head back and inhaled deeply; the air was so different, touching her face with the clean, sweet smell of autumn.

The wheel lurched and her chair rocked on its hinges, bringing a quiet smile to her face. Higher it rolled until she could see out over the tops of the tents, beyond the bend in the bay where the big ships loaded grain. She could feel the life of all she beheld while looking out across the green hills to the mountains, a sense that the world that was reaching out to her. The seat jerked again.

She glanced down. The wheel jockey was holding his hands like a megaphone to his lips. Dessie waved back without uttering a sound. Her mind was too busy absorbing the scene spreading out before her eyes to care what he was shouting up to her. Her gazing out over the harbor became a mystic message, holding her attention transfixed to the infinite view of the sky and the sea. Suddenly, her bucket seat began to drop as the wheel rotated, taking her down past the engine in a sweeping motion, past the wheel jockey on the platform and then rising once more.

Dessie felt her soul being lifted up; her view, a look at the world surrounding her she had never before seen. Then she sensed the world dropping away and she was on her way down a second time, suddenly remembering her promise to the wheel jockey to holler. But it was too late. She got as far as inhaling a breath, but the wheel had stopped before she could utter a sound.

"What's the matter? What happened?" The red-faced, angry wheel jockey demanded.

"I forgot," she said lamely.

"Forgot? I even shook the wheel. You and me, we made a deal. Right?" He grumbled, slamming open the safety bar. "Get your ass out of my Ferris wheel."

"I'm sorry," she muttered.

"As far as I'm concerned, you owe me two bits. Either pay like everybody else or get outta my sight." The girl rubbed her hands nervously over her hips. "I don't have any money," she confessed. "It felt so good up there, that I forgot everything you said."

The wheel jockey shook his head and started the engine, the wheel beginning the lazy, slow climb back up until it seemed to touch the sky. Dessie stood watching her empty blue chair as it rose, recalling the touch of the cool breeze and the quiet voice of the stillness that had possessed her at the summit.

Isaiah, waiting for his mother in the open-top 1916 twin-six Packard parked alongside the Wolfe & Bloomberg department store, was watching the girl on the Ferris wheel. She was the only passenger to ride in the thirty minutes he had been watching. He found himself wondering what it would be like, soaring over the shore on the Ferris wheel.

As he watched the girl step off the wheel and being confronted by the wheel jockey, something, perhaps it was simply his curiosity, made him lean forward to speak to the chauffeur.

"George," he said, from the back seat. "I'm going to walk

down to that street fair. When my mother returns, you can come and pick me up."

The chauffeur, one of the few who understood the mechanics and who could drive the new horseless carriages, got out of the car to protest. It was his responsibility to watch over the boy. "I better come along with you, lad," he suggested, aware of how upset the boy's mother would be if she were to learn that her son had been permitted to wander the downtown streets on his own. Mingling with who knows what types of street people?

"No. You wait for mother in the car," Isaiah instructed. He had that kind of authority about him even as a teenaged child. "Come and pick me up when she returns. I intend to stay in plain sight where you can keep an eye on me."

Arriving at the fair, Isaiah remained at a distance watching the confrontation between the wheel jockey and the girl. When the man finally turned away, Isaiah approached Dessie, shaking his head ruefully.

"You don't get it," he said to the girl. "That guy was expecting you to be a shill."

"What's that?" She asked, turning to face this strange boy wearing a St. George's School blazer and well-pressed, grey-flannel shorts.

"You were supposed to act as if you were excited, or thrilled when you got to the top. That guy wanted you to show something that would make the others interested in getting on the wheel," Isaiah answered, casually continuing to wipe the cotton candy from his fingers with a pristine white handkerchief.

"But I was enjoying the ride. It was thrilling," Dessie insisted, aware from the minute their eyes met there was something about this strange boy that fascinated her. It wasn't anything physical, neither Isaiah nor the girl had experienced those feelings the day they first met. But there was something familiar about the easy flow of their conversation that would have caused an observer to believe they had known one another a long time. There was no getting-to-know-you introduction, nothing to indicate they were two strangers meeting for the first time.

"That's what being a shill means," Isaiah explained. "You become the Judas goat, the one that leads the sheep to slaughter. If you had been hollering up there on the wheel the customers would have lined up ready to pay for a ride on his broken-down Ferris wheel."

"It wasn't broken down at all," Dessie argued. "The man asked me to pretend I was scared. But I wasn't. When I was up there at the top, it was like I was flying," she said. "He never said anything about me being a Judas goat either."

"You want to ride again?" Isaiah asked abruptly.

Dessie shrugged. "The man says I owe him twenty-five cents for the ride I already had. And I don't have twenty-five cents."

Isaiah beckoned to the wheel jockey, who reluctantly shuffled over. He handed the man a fifty cent piece. "That's twenty-five cents for the ride she took, and twenty-five for the ride she's going to take now. That's better than twice your regular fare," he added, indicating the advertised price per ride as ten cents.

The wheel jockey stared at the fifty-cent piece in his hand and smiled a soiled smile, exposing food particles wedged in his yellow teeth. "How's about you both taking a ride, together? I'll make it two for the price of one. Might be good for business."

Isaiah replied with a negative shake of his head. "Just the girl."

"Oh please come," Dessie urged. "It's not scary. You can see forever up there. I won't go, unless you come with me."

Isaiah had never been on a Ferris wheel, had never tasted cotton candy, either. This was his first visit to any kind of a street fair. And when Dessie reached for his hand urging him toward the wheel, he discovered he was suddenly sharing this impish thirteen-year-old girl's excitement at the prospect of riding this questionable wheel.

It was a strange decision for young Isaiah. He had been convinced since he was three or four that he was the possessor of a strong self-will. And yet here he was being crammed into the bucket seat of the Ferris wheel with this girl's thigh pressing against his leg, the two of them squeezed into the swaying bucket.

For Isaiah, it was a terrorizing ride, the bucket threatening to dump the two of them out at any minute. Dessie saw his fear and reached for his hand.

"It gets better when we get to the top," she promised. "Wait 'till he stops the wheel. You'll see."

It was true. Isaiah did manage to catch his breath as the breeze off the bay touched his cheek. Yet as refreshing as the wind felt on his face, in his mind their bucket seat was still dangerously rocking in the breeze. All the while, he continued clinging with one hand to the reassurance of Dessie's hand, while with the other gripping the lap bar that was supposed to be securing their place in the rocking bucket seat.

"My name is Desdemona Patricia Gonne. Some of the kids at school call me Patricia. I hate that. Patricia is my middle name. The Nuns all call me Dessie. You can call me Desdemona, if you like." The girl was chatting aimlessly, hoping that once she started him talking he would relax and be less afraid. It was very apparent Isaiah was regretting his ever agreeing to join her ride.

Isaiah, his mind somewhere between catching the view out over the bay and his concern over the dangers of the rocking of the bucket seat, failed to answer.

"My mother named me. She read the name Desdemona on a sign; one of those they paste to telephone poles? It was advertising a play, by Shakespeare, I think. My mother thought with a name like Desdemona, I could do great things with my life. She decided on the name. She even had it written out without even knowing she was having a girl. Just think if I had been a boy, with a name like Desdemona." Dessie rattled on, sensing her chatter was helping to relax her new-found friend.

Isaiah nodded, keeping his eyes fixed on the horizon, hoping the view would keep his mind off the prospect of falling the fifty feet they would drop to the earth if tipped out of the rocking bucket seat. "Isaiah," he muttered.

"Isaiah?" The girl repeated the name as a question.

"That's my name. Isaiah," he repeated.

"That's a biblical name. Isaiah was one of the prophets in the Old Testament. That means you have been sent by an angel to remind me that I need to do my Catechism homework," she laughed. "I don't really know much about Isaiah. But I'm going to find out," she promised.

The wheel lurched and Isaiah reached anxiously for her hand again. Dessie smiled reassuringly. "Keep looking over the bay," she said calmly. "The view will steal your mind. It did mine."

They were on their second whirl into the air and Isaiah was beginning to relax with the ride when he looked to the ground to see the Wolfe family Packard arriving at the curb below. Rosa Wolfe was out of the car before the wheel circled up once more.

"That's my son you have up there. Bring him down, at once," she commanded.

Isaiah quickly let go of Dessie's hand. "Where do you go to school?" he asked in something of a whisper.

"Our Lady of Perpetual Help," Dessie answered. "I'm in the seventh grade." She had not finished answering before Rosa lifted the lap bar that had them fastened in the seat.

"Come along son," Rosa said with a forced smile for the girl. "Mother is sorry she took so long. Say goodbye to this nice girl. George wants to start for home before the traffic gets terrible."

CHAPTER 7: DEATH OF THE PATRIARCH

Asa Wolfe stood quietly in the cover of the passage behind the freight elevator, having hidden there to observe the idling workers on the loading dock. When he could no longer stand what he saw, he stepped into the midst of the gossiping crew.

"Gentlemen. Just what is it you are doing here?" he asked with ironic softness. "I have been watching you for fifteen minutes and I haven't been able to tell what it is that you are being paid for?" I gather you are not unloading, because I have yet to see a single box unloaded from a truck or a wagon in the past quarter of an hour that I have been watching you."

One burly teamster, failing to recognize the little man who was posing the question, smirked. "You might say we are just fucking the dog."

"And do you know who I am? I happen to be the dog you are fucking," Asa screamed. With that, he took off his suit coat, tossing it to the dock floor and ferociously began attacking the pile of boxes on the nearest wagon. He was throwing the boxes onto the dock, some missing the mark and falling to the road below, bursting open as they landed around the feet of the stunned workers. Asa worked furiously for a full minute or two when suddenly he stopped, his face drained of color and now wet with sweat. Pulling at his collar, he leaned back against the pile of unloaded boxes, with a pleading whisper sinking to his knees. He uttered one word. "Water." It was the last word Asa Wolfe ever spoke. He was sixty.

Asa Wolfe's body was carried to his home in a company truck plainly marked with the Wolfe & Bloomberg initials and bearing the dark blue colors of the store. When the doctor called from the hospital to inform her of her husband's death, Rosa ordered a company truck to pick up the body, refusing to allow them to take him to the mortuary. What the morticians would do for him, they would do in his own home beneath her watchful eye.

Asa's body was placed on a table in the open foyer at the foot of the sweeping stairwell where the undertakers came to dress him for the official mourning.

Rosa called for a chair to be set beside the table where the undertakers laid him out and undressed him, carefully removing what remained of his clothes, to begin washing his nude body. They bathed his wrinkled knees and wiped the body fluids from his thighs, rolling him to one side to get at the body waste that had escaped. Rosa never glanced away, instructing them on how to comb his thinning grey hair and it was she who set his thin lips in a semblance of a smile. They dressed him in a stiff black suit, awkwardly lifting his naked limbs under the fixed stare of the widow.

During his lifetime, Asa was the unchallenged power of the big store, and the entire world – as Asa had known it – came to pay its respects. The mayor, the councilmen, and two senators, all in tall hats and beaver collars, each unctuously recalling the help and leadership of the Jew who had intimidated them in life and now lay neutered by death in the front hall. The scent of dying flowers drenched the house in a pungent perfume that mixed with the fruit and cakes and tokens of obeisance from farmers, hot houses, stores, and strangers the Wolfes had never known. Through it all Isaiah looked up into the endless line of passing faces, most of them glancing down skeptically on his tiny presence.

"You have big shoes to fill, young man. Some day you may grow up to be half the man your father was." Some even likened him to his father, marveling with Rosa at Isaiah's physical resemblance to his father, as much to assure her that they accepted Asa's role in the boy's creation, as it was acknowledging the presence of his father's large nose. Asa was buried that same day.

Ten days after all of this had passed, Isaiah, wearing a tightly fitted grey suit and a large blue bow tie, with a black arm band on his sleeve, followed his mother into the big store.

Nathan Bloomberg was there to meet them on the executive floor, preening behind his drooping mustache, his shoulders squared to the world, a monstrous elk's tooth dangling from the double breasted vest that covered the expanse of his belly. He smelled of cigars and took Rosa' hands and pulled her into his arms.

"Rosa. It's so good to see you up and about. You will take comfort, I know, to learn we have touched nothing in Asa' office since the day he left us. Except for a few papers, you will find things as he left them. Consider the office your office and Isaiah's, whenever the boy is ready to step in to help us out."

Rosa thanked them in a manner that was more a reconnaissance of their attitude than gratitude, her manner designed to let them know she was not a helpless widow, and that she would be present to protect her interest and her son's future.

Asa's 'particular papers,' as he called his hand-scribbled notes and personal papers, were stuffed into his desk, to which he alone carried the keys. Those keys had been held by Rosa since they undressed Asa's body before her eyes. Asa would lock that desk even if it was merely to go to the toilet. Rosa didn't miss any of this as she waited for the Bloombergs to leave.

"Wc would like to be alone with his things for a while," she finally said, smiling Nathan and Jake from the office. When they were gone, she turned to the desk and slid open the drawer. It was unlocked, and Asa's papers were gone.

CHAPTER 8: THE BEACH HOUSE

The following year, Isaiah was excited to be driving to the beach. Alex Burns, Rosa's newly hired chauffeur, had convinced her to trade the 1915 Packard for a new Cadillac. This was the boy's first summer at the beach without the prospect of having his father intruding with his inquisitional type of accountability.

When still alive, Asa had been in the habit of arriving on the late Saturday afternoon train, storming into the cocoon-like warmth and security Rosa built around her son during their week alone at the beach house. Asa's arrival would immediately set about disrupting the summer place in a manner that would leave his presence felt all throughout the following week.

On busy weekends, when the store had a big promotion, the old man would not arrive until the Sunday morning train. On those weekends, he used to announce his arrival by barging into his son's bedroom in the morning, or awaken him by slamming doors and complaining in a loud voice that nobody cared that it was he who was providing the bread for the table of this house. Until first the cook, and then Rosa and his son, would join him at the kitchen table, still wearing their night clothes.

The three of them would then watch while the cook served him tea in a tall glass, which he drank with one spoon left in the glass to prevent its cracking, while scolding each of them on general principles. Eventually he would curl up on a sofa, snoring loudly throughout the morning. When he awoke, he would begin his sessions of accountability for the events of the week past.

The session Isaiah remembered most vividly was the day he happened to be on the upstairs porch dropping a kitten over the railing, feet raised to the sky, to see if the cat would land on its feet as he had been told. It did. His father, who was ensconced in the big chair overlooking the sand dunes and the beach pines stretching to the shore, seeing the kitten flying past the porch, hollered for his son.

"Isaiah." Asa's thin voice would echo throughout the house. Seeing the boy appear, he would indicate with the familiarity of an unspoken command for him to take a seat on his lap.

"Now, what's all this I hear about your goings-on. I have been told what you have been up to this past week." It was the old man's technique, developed in the store for making the person being questioned believe that he knew something, without ever revealing what he knew, if anything.

In the beginning, Isaiah invented stories of the cook's feeding the man who came with firewood for the house. That appeared to bore Asa. Then the boy added the scene of the woodman, with his pecker in his hand, pissing against the garage, then waving his pecker for Isaiah to see. That impressed the old man so much it provided the boy a cue that led to his fictional confessions of the fat, middle-aged cook drinking beer in her underwear in the kitchen. "And she let me touch her milkers," Isaiah confessed in feigned guilt that pleased the old man even more.

Isaiah began to play the game with a perverse understanding of the needs of his father. "I was looking at the cook when she was all bare," he confessed in a later session.

"Yes. Yes," his father urged, the post-nap glaze having settled over the old man's eyes. "And then what did you do?"

The boy stammered in feigned guilt. "I was hiding in her closet." The old man's fist gripped his arm until Isaiah grimaced.

"You are not telling me the truth. You must trust me. I am your father. Tell me what you did and it will be better for you."

"I fell asleep, in the closet," the boy said.

"You lie. You did not fall asleep. You are not telling me what happened, what you were thinking when you saw her naked. Until you tell me about yourself, I cannot trust you. You can never be me unless I trust you. I know about young boys. I already know what it is that you are not telling me. Trust me," whispered the old man, "all I am asking is that you should trust me."

Isaiah then invented tales of how he had put his prick in the cook's teacup and pressed it against the cold china, rubbing it against the lip of the cup before placing the cup back on the shelf.

"I was watching her when she put the cup to her lips. I was afraid she would smell me," he told his father. "Then I stayed in the toilet to make myself feel good. But it didn't make me feel good, Poppa. It made me feel sick in my stomach, like I might vomit," he blurted. It was a convincing story, and Asa Wolfe leaned back in his chair believing his son.

"Now I know you have told me the truth. I want you to tell me about your mother too. And the cook. I want to know you are telling me everything."

"Yes, Poppa." And that remained the pattern, summer after summer until the year Asa died, but not before Rosa sensed the need to intervene.

"Your father doesn't need to know every little detail of what goes on here," Rosa explained one Monday following Asa's returning to the store. "It's all right if you tell him some little things that would be useful for him to know. But remember, your father has lots to worry about in the business. He doesn't need to be worried about what happens here. Do you understand me?"

Isaiah understood.

CHAPTER 9:

DESDEMONA PATRICIA GONNE

It was spring, and the early morning dew came seeping through Dessie Gonne's canvas tennis shoes. The dampness at her toes seemed to spread through her shivering body as she pulled her fists inside the sleeves of her cotton sweater. Glancing down at her four-year-old brother, she asked: "What did you do with our lunch?"

"I forgot," the boy confessed.

A look of sudden desperation revealed the indecision rushing through the teenaged girl's mind. She was calculating the time it would take to run home to retrieve the brown paper lunch sack, against her chances of missing the bus and the entire day in the berry fields. The boy had asked if he could carry the lunch, and she had felt good giving him that responsibility.

"I told you, again and again. Don't forget the lunch," she said, swiftly pulling free from her sweater jacket and handing it to the boy. "Wait here." She whirled and started the run for home. In that same instant the berry farm's yellow-and-black retired school bus appeared around the corner. Dessie was in mid-stride when she caught sight of the bus and stopped, hurrying back to the boy as the bus pulled up to the curb.

"Bailey's Berry Farm?" The woman driver leaned her elbow on the wheel impatiently. The thin-faced girl nodded and pushed the boy's shoulder, urging him up the bus steps. The woman shook her head watching the pair climb aboard before slamming the door. "They aren't going to allow that kid into the fields," she warned.

Taking their seat, Dessie glanced nervously over her shoulder at two Japanese teenagers seated in the back before she began scolding the boy in a forced whisper. "You expect me to remember everything? You wanted to carry the lunch. You even..." Her voice trailed off, her anger dying at the look on the pale, silent face beside her. The boy stared down at his shoes.

"What are we going to eat?" he asked plaintively.

"We will find something," Dessie replied.

"Star berries," the boy answered hopefully.

"You mean straw-berries." She smiled.

"I like star berries."

"Too many strawberries will make you sick unless you eat a sandwich with them," she said, her voice softening.

"And water. They got water for us," the boy added.

Dessie moved closer and put an arm over his shoulder, sharing the frail warmth of her body in the cold jostling bus that smelt of sour sweat and exhaust fumes coming up through the floor. They rode on silently, the bus cruising through side streets, picking up more kids and one middle-aged couple carrying a pot and a black, metal lunch pail.

The chatting passengers grew quiet when the bus turned into the dirt tracks leading through the lush-green berry fields, and lurched to a stop. Dessie and her brother stepped down alongside a teetering stack of berry crates. "Stay near me and don't open your mouth," the girl whispered, taking the boy's hand.

A heavy-set woman, seated on the edge of a badly worn leather chair alongside a stack of empty crates, looked up from her list of pickers. Dessie told the keeper of the weights her name.

"Gonne. Dessie. I got it," the woman said. "And what'd'ya expect to do with him?" She demanded.

"He's my brother. I have to look after him," Dessie said. "He's going to help me."

"Why can't I pick myself?" the boy whispered.

"What's that?" The woman leaned forward to catch what the boy had whispered.

The boy slipped further behind his sister. "He's going to help me," Dessie said again. She picked up a number from the box on the table and helped herself to an empty berry flat from the stack.

"He's too young," the woman said. "We can't let kids into the fields. They cause too much trouble." The girl looked at the woman with a silent blank stare that lasted a long moment. "Well," the woman sighed. "If you promise to keep an eye on the kid and keep him outta the way of the pickers, I suppose it will be okay for today. See that he don't start throwing berries around, or out you go. Both of you."

By mid-morning the heat from the sun had grown hot on her back when Dessie straightened up, bracing one berry-stained hand on her hip. She brushed the loose strands of ginger-colored hair from her face and turned, searching the field for her brother. He stood right behind her. The boy's face was creased with a smile that looked as if it had been painted on with berry juice. He had a look on his face that made her think of a puppy dog pleading for an ear rubbing. He came toward her tray with a handful of berries for her empty basket. "You hungry?" she asked.

"Uh uh," the boy answered. "I ate all the berries I could." She smiled at him and resumed working her fingers beneath the bushes. She picked straddling the rows, bending to brush the leaves aside in search of the berries. Though the mid-day sun continued to grow hotter throughout the afternoon, Dessie Gonne was the last picker to leave the field that day. She was also the last to have her card total recorded by the woman in the leather chair.

"I see you had a good day," the woman in the chair said counting up her tally. "The kid brother help much?"

Dessie shook her head and shrugged. "Could I have a dollar today?" she asked.

"Why? Are you quitting?" The woman was afraid of losing her good pickers.

"No. I just need a dollar."

"You understand, Saturday is the day you get paid for the entire week? What do you want the dollar for?"

"Lunch," Dessie said.

"Lunch? It's near dinner time. Didn't you get enough to eat out there?"

The bus driver beeped the horn, impatient to get started.

"Here," the woman said, producing a dollar bill from the pocket of her smock. "That comes off your card, you understand."

On the bus with the late afternoon sun beating through the dirty glass windows, the boy shut his eyes, his tongue raw and tasteless from the strawberries. "Can we open the window?" he asked.

Dessie struggled with the window, until the man who had boarded the bus in the morning with his wife reached over the boy and forced open the window. The boy grinned at the touch of the warm, late-afternoon air rushing through the opening and closed his eyes. In the red darkness appearing in his vision, he saw strawberries, strawberries and more strawberries, all the same size, rolling and tumbling, one atop another. "I think I might be sick," he said.

***

Desdemona Patricia Gonne's mother, Mary Louise Ryan, died of tuberculosis when Dessie was thirteen years old. Her mother's second child, Andrew, was born three years before she died. The children's father, Sergeant Major Harold Gonne, a World War I veteran, managed to leave his widow and two children a modest 'army benefit' house and what remained of his pension. He died from the after-effects of German mustard gas a year before his wife's passing.

Shortly following the sergeant major's death, Seamus Ryan, Mary Louise's alcoholic new husband, moved in with the family. Ryan's purported marriage to Mary Louise was reportedly an unorthodox ceremony conducted by a woman preacher, who never asked to see the marriage license.

Unfortunately for Ryan, the house was tied up in the children's names, though he wasted no time in using Mary Louise's death, and what resources of hers he could lay his hands on, as his reason for drowning what was left of his life in alcohol. And when whiskey was unobtainable, rubbing alcohol, hair tonic or after-shave lotion would do. Andrew was able to recall a day in his teens when his surrogate stepfather squeezed a can of shoe polish through a stocking in his thirst for alcohol. It was neighborhood knowledge that when their ersatz stepfather showed up at the house, Dessie and Andrew left to stay with their mother's sister.

This dysfunctional family structure cast Dessie in the role of mother to her young brother. She taught him to use the toilet until he could do his business on his own. She changed and washed his diapers until he was three. Dessie began taking him with her into the berry fields when the boy was four, and by the time he was twelve, Andrew was matching her berry for berry. He was sixteen when he began to exhibit his stepfather's craving for alcohol and landed in trouble.

His crime? In his search for money to bargain for beer, Andrew took to canvassing the neighborhood in the pre-dawn darkness to steal the nickels and dimes from milk bottles left on the porches for the milk delivery wagon. When neighbors grew concerned and the milkman stopped leaving fresh quarts of milk, a neighborhood night watchman, returning home early, stationed himself behind the curtains of his living room. The watchman was watching from behind the curtain when Andrew crept onto his porch and emptied two dimes from the milk bottle. The boy ran, but the night watchman had recognized him and called the police.

The following afternoon, a police sergeant came knocking on the Gonne front door. The policeman, introducing himself, explained that he too was an Irish Catholic and had known, if somewhat vaguely, the late Sergeant Major Harry Gonne. With that out of the way, he coughed into his fist.

"We have learned that you have a lad in this house that is

wanted by the police," he informed Dessie, who stood shielding her sixteen-year-old brother behind the partially opened door.

"Can you tell me what this is all about?" Dessie asked.

"No. That I cannot. But if you turn him over to me with no trouble, I'll not be informing the welfare office of your living here alone with the boy with no adult supervision; at least none that I can see," the sergeant replied.

"I'm twenty-six," Dessie interrupted.

"All I am permitted to say to you is that there has been a complaint filed charging the lad with larceny. That's thievery, a serious crime."

"Is there some way we can replace what he has taken," the girl pleaded. "He told me it was the change from the neighbors' milk bottles."

"The boy must appear to answer the charge," the sergeant replied sternly. "Now, if he is standing behind that door, and I suspect he is, you would do well to turn him over to me. Let the lad tell his side of the story to the juvenile court."

Dessie was aware of the possibility that their erstwhile guardian and ersatz stepfather, Seamus Ryan, could show up at any moment, drunk. She was not about to have the policeman meet the man whom the Welfare Office regarded as the family's stabilizing influence. Turning to Andrew, she managed a smile, hoping to add a measure of confidence that everything would be worked out.

"I'm afraid, little brother, you are going to have to go with the policeman. We don't want your stepfather involved in this. He has already caused us troubles enough."

The sergeant pushed open the door and took Andrew by the shoulder. "You'll need a lawyer if you expect to bring the boy home without his doing some serious time or ending up a ward of the Juvenile Court," he said, his voice softening at the sight of a cowering Andrew. "Do you have anyone? Someone you can trust who understands what you are dealing with now that the Sergeant Major is gone?"

"No," Dessie said with a note of defeat.

"There's a young lad, not long out of law school. His name is Patrick Higgins. He has no office to speak of, but you can catch up to him in the County Courthouse in the morning. He is there every morning looking for an appointment by the court or looking for clients. You could do worse. He's an Irish Mick as well."

With that, the sergeant steered Andrew to the waiting police car, pausing to shout back over his shoulder. "Don't you be worrying about your brother, young lady. A couple of nights in the Juvenile Detention Center will do him no harm, and maybe teach him to have some respect for other people's milk bottle money."

Dessie was in the County Courthouse long before the first morning traffic session was called to order. She had found a seat in the back of the court when the judge looked up from the bench.

"Higgins?" the judge called out. "Where is that law-school kid, Pat Higgins?"

A burly figure with a mop of black hair raised his hand and Patrick Higgins approached the bench. There followed a brief interlude while the traffic judge conferred with the lawyer about a pending case. When the judge seemed satisfied with Higgins' proposed adjournment, the lawyer gathered up his papers and was about to leave the courtroom. Dessie Gonne stood in his way.

"Please, Mister Higgins, have you a minute to spare?"

Higgins shrugged, looking up from the bundle of papers tucked beneath his arm. He decided he was facing what he judged to be a nineteen- or twenty-year- old girl. "My time is your time," he said lightly, quoting, with a trace of melody, the Rudy Vallee ballad. "Let's step outside the courtroom, so we don't upset the judge."

"It is about my brother," she said as they huddled in the hallway. "He was arrested yesterday morning."

"In that case," Higgins answered, "he is probably still in jail. Right?"

"He is in the Juvenile Detention Center. He is sixteen years old," the girl answered.

Higgins, fresh out of law school, newly married, and pretty much flat broke, sighed. "Maybe we should step outside. We can talk on the Courthouse steps. You never know who is listening to the whispers in a Courthouse hall," he said, steering the girl through the doorway onto the stone steps outside.

"I can afford to take you for a cup of coffee and I have some money to pay you for your time," the girl said. "If you have the time?"

Higgins continued to smile. "I thought I had made that clear. Time is what I have. Clients are what I am looking for."

Over coffee, Dessie spelled out the details of her plight, laying out the Gonne family history, including the role of her late mother's live-in boyfriend, who passed as the family's surrogate head of the family. Higgins listened, quickly grasping the story.

"I'd say we have two, maybe three problems," he said. "One is getting the boy out of the detention facility. Two is keeping the Child Welfare people from putting the boy in a foster home. And three; how much money do you have to pay me?"

"Enough to pay for the coffee and maybe a little bit more," the girl replied cautiously.

"I like the sound of your case and you have my sympathy," Higgins replied. "But I can't afford to work for coffee. How much can you pay me?" he repeated.

"I have close to three hundred dollars, mostly berry picking money, though I have been working part time at Wolfe & Bloomberg for going on three years," she answered.

"And still part time?" Higgins asked.

"If it is more than that, I promise I will pay you the rest when..." She stammered, embarrassed to be begging this stranger who stood listening with a steady smile on his face. She drew in her breath and straightened her shoulders.

"I am going to have pay for my brother to be admitted to an alcohol treatment," she said with renewed confidence. "You can trust me to pay the rest of what I owe you, later."

The lawyer nodded, studying this ginger-haired girl who made him feel that he was dealing with a nineteen-year-old Orphan Annie. "How about you paying me fifty dollars up front, and I will do what I can on behalf of your brother. You say they picked him up yesterday? And he is being held in juvenile detention. I can check the charges and see if we can get him released this afternoon."

Higgins, pinching his chin between his thumb and forefinger, assumed the pose of man pondering a decision without ever losing his smile. "I will have to work things out with the Welfare people," he said thinking aloud. "That's a half a day or more. Say, another hundred dollars." He studied her face as the girl wrestled with her finances.

"And you can pay me when you have the money," he announced. "Your brother apparently has an affliction common to the Irish, with which I happen to be familiar. It's important that he gets treatment while he's young."

Dessie paid the fifty dollars, two twenties and a ten, and Andrew was released to Higgins' custody that afternoon. She was waiting for the two of them on the steps of the Juvenile Court when they appeared, Andrew looking harried and unwashed. Higgins, with one arm over the shoulder of her brother, was grinning triumphantly. She and Andrew rode the streetcar home.

Dessie paid two hundred and fifty dollars of the three hundred she had in savings to the General Hospital and signed her name on a pledge to pay the balance in installments.

CHAPTER10:

THE AUSTRIAN BOYS SCHOOL

The new Cadillac had been rolling westward, over the twisting two-lane highway alongside the swiftly moving river for an hour or more. They had driven past the marshlands into the slopes of the Coast Range where the stands of Douglas Firs form a canyon on either side of the road for the remainder of the hundred miles to the beach. The family baggage was following in a separate van. There was only the mother and her son in the glassed-off rear compartment of the large automobile.

Isaiah felt the comfort of her body next to him on the plush seat, though he was puzzled why the cook wasn't with them. Rosa had instructed the cook to come with the van bringing the supplies. If there wasn't room in the van, she was to follow on the Monday morning train. Usually cook would ride with the family in the train and play cards with Isaiah or polish his nails or teach him to knit while Rosa tried to sleep.

Isaiah knew when his mother announced that they were going to take the new car to the beach, that she had something on her mind. He thought he recognized what it was when, after a long silence, she asked innocently, "Isaiah. Do you remember, before your father died, when you were with that girl on the Ferris wheel?"

Isaiah shrugged. "Don't remember."

"Did you like her?" Rosa pressed on.

"She was all right, I suppose," he answered casually.

"I thought I overheard you asking her name?"

"Don't remember," he said.

"Oh yes you do," Rosa said in a teasing voice. "Now I'm

beginning to worry why you wouldn't want to tell me?"

"Her name was Desdemona Gonne," Rosa said with a smile that said, 'you can't keep secrets from me!' "I overheard her telling you."

There followed a long moment of silence broken only by the soft purr of the Packard engine until Rosa spoke again.

"Gonne. That's Irish, isn't it? I also heard her tell you she went to a Catholic school."

Isaiah shrugged indifferently. There followed another long pause before Rosa Wolfe spoke again. "You know, if you have an interest in girls, your father would have approved, providing the girl was Jewish. This girl is an Irish Catholic."

"I'm not interested," Isaiah replied.

"Well then, I have a question for you. How would you like to visit Europe this fall?" his mother finally asked.

"With you?" Isaiah asked, immediately suspicious of her seeking his opinion.

"Of course with me. Do you think I would send you away without me?" She laughed.

Still, he was distrustful. Rosa had picked up the technique of answering a question with a question, a practice of her late husband. It had served as Asa's means of evading an answer. When Isaiah refused to say anything further, but sat quietly waiting for the rest of what she had to say, Rosa blurted out the reason for her question.

"I am taking you to school in Austria this fall. The same school your father attended when he was a boy your age."

"But I don't want to go to Austria. Why do you want to get rid of me? I don't want to be that far away from the business. Poppa would not want that."

"There are times in a boy's life when he should get out in the world with other boys," Rosa answered. "It is time for you to begin to learn things about the world beyond the store."

"Learn things?" Isaiah laughed disparagingly with a sniff. "I can learn everything I need to know right here, with you," he answered, aware that to argue with his mother was pointless. Still he pressed on. "Poppa taught me all about people. He taught me about you and the chauffer and the clerks in the store." The color began to rise in Rosa's face, and he hesitated, realizing this was not the time for that kind of confrontation.

"What do you mean? What did he teach you about me?"

"He taught me about Jews and Goyim, and how you manage to get along with everyone, even Presbyterians, like Alex," Isaiah said, slipping free of the noose he had momentarily hung around his own neck.

Rosa had heard enough. She inhaled deeply, signaling their conversation was finished. Then, smiling her motherly smile, she announced, "It is all settled. We leave in September." She then quickly pretended to fall asleep, her fine bosom rising and falling in rhythmic breathing beneath the silk ruffle of her blouse. Isaiah and his mother sailed for Europe that fall and he was enrolled in the Austrian school for boys.

***

It was four years before he returned home from Europe, four years of learning the absolute separateness that constantly haunted a Jew in one of Europe's most expensive schools. While there were one or two other Jewish boys in the school, those four years were Isaiah's introduction to the chilling class snobbery of European families with titles in their ancestry, regardless of how ephemeral the titles turned out to be. Some possessed greater wealth than anyone he knew. It was an education taught and maintained with canings and cricket-field honor, which for Isaiah was no honor at all. He learned these lessons painfully, secretly filing those experiences into the fabric of his thinking. But while he railed at the discipline leveled by senior boys, he also learned to play that game and became just one of the wealthy American Jews abroad.

While at school, Isaiah attended services in the Lutheran chapel and took communion with his classmates and he told stories about the 'Kikes' his father had known in America. He even laughed with the others when they told and retold the story of his having sat in a tree all night long to escape a caning with the prefect, who had watched from the chapel window to see if he would fall asleep and drop out of the tree. He didn't. He remained seated in the tree until the school sent for his mother from Bludenz the following morning. She begged him to come down at once. He did and was caned and confined to his dorm, and was caned again for leaving it without permission.

School in Austria began to come to an end for Isaiah in his fourth year, when he decided on his own it was time for him to leave. He insulted a prefect, refused his punishment and walked alone into the village of Bludenz, where he took up rooms in a family hotel, bought his own meals and ignored the delegation that arrived at his hotel to return him to school.

This open challenge to school authority was a new experience for the institution and they handled it awkwardly, hiring the village constabulary to return him bodily to the dorm. Immediately following his return and the usual caning, a fire broke out in Isaiah's dormitory and the school discovered the near terrifying resolve behind those black, secretive eyes.

The school could never be certain it was Isaiah who started the fire, though he was there, trotting out onto the lawn with the others at the first sound of the alarm, and watching the east end of the building burn to the ground. But when they questioned him, Isaiah, wise in his father's ways, denied with candid calmness that he had anything to do with the blaze. And until the following December when his mother would arrive to take him to Paris for the winter holidays, the school offered their American student a wide berth.

But he was not yet free. It required one last brutal demonstration of private school depravity to open the doors that would release him. It came as a result of a confrontation with a prefect assigning Isaiah the chore of polishing the cricket team trophies that were proudly displayed under glass in the school rotunda. Isaiah was not a cricket player. He was bored with the slow-moving game, and when he suggested a member of the cricket team should polish the silver, the prefect merely replied: "I have ordered you to polish the trophies. And you will. Now make them shine."

To which Isaiah replied with a terse: "Why don't you kiss my ass?"

Summoned to the provost's office, he found himself facing the tall, thin provost, and Englishman with the name John Wickham, who greeted him smiling ominously from behind his desk.

"Isaiah Wolfe," the provost began, "this school has been embarrassed by your behavior. You have refused to accept decent discipline like a man, so now you will accept it like a child." Two of the larger senior boys then entered the office, took Isaiah's hands and feet and proceeded to bend him across the edge of the desk. They then pulled down his trousers, and the caning by John Wickham began with the perverted sadism of the time and place that was then leveled at boys with nowhere to turn.

When John Wickham had finished, a fine sweat breaking out over his brow from the considerable exertion of the caning, he granted Isaiah permission to raise his trousers. As he reached for the trousers, which had fallen to his ankles, the bleeding from the canning came seeping through the white linen.

Unfortunately for the school, Rosa Wolfe arrived unannounced from Paris that afternoon and Isaiah was summoned, limping into the provost's office, to greet his mother and to answer for his rebellious behavior. He hobbled painfully into the room, and without speaking a word, silently lowered his knickers exposing the welts on his naked, bleeding buttocks to his mother.

Isaiah knew her well, knew her animal instincts and the protectiveness of her one surviving child that was always lurking near the surface of her seemingly calm exterior. Rosa, seeing the still bloody wounds, screamed in a voice that echoed through every building on the quad; her cry sounding as if the cane had landed across her breasts.

She rose up out of her chair, charging like an angry mother bear attacking a hunter at the sight of her injured cub. "You sonovabitch," she cried. "What kind of fucking Inquisition is it you are running in this shithouse of a school?"

The provost, an agile academic, recoiled in fear, quickly ducking behind his large desk to escape her charge, and fled, terrified that in her fury the woman was about to tear him limb from limb.

When she had finished with them, and they were certain her solicitors were soon to follow, she took Isaiah to a hotel in the village where she bathed him in Epsom salts. Though the boy was years past puberty, she handled him as an infant babe, lifting him bodily in and out of the large porcelain tub, gently swabbing the whipping wounds with fresh linen-soaked ointment.

Following six days of a hurried Atlantic crossing, and three days out of Boston on the trans-continental Union Pacific, they were met at the train by Alex, the family chauffeur with the Packard. It was six days before Christmas, the landscape barren and cold. It had been snowing through the night and the first warmth of the morning was turning the light flurries into a fine, chilling mist. On the drive up to the house, Isaiah smiled at the sight of the melting snow piled in large heaps to the side of the driveway. The grounds keepers had arisen early with the news of their homecoming and had shoveled the entire long driveway clean. For Isaiah, the puddles that lay in patches across the lawns, and the chill of late December, and the naked tree branches in sterile relief against the grey sky, meant only that he was home at last. He was overcome, his tears freely coursing down his cheeks, on viewing the home he had not seen for four years.

And while wrapped beneath the Packard driving blanket, his

mind was busy at work on his plans to return to the store. Even before leaving Europe, he announced to his mother his intention of assuming a position in the store. "That is where I belong and that is where Poppa would want me to be. I never did understand why we had to go through that European school business in the first place" he scolded her.

Rosa had listened to his complaints all across the Atlantic and through three days and nights aboard the train, without ever revealing her feelings. Isaiah reminded her again and again of the need to protect their interest at the store, telling her unsavory stories gathered from his father about the activities of the Bloombergs, father and son. "How can we trust our interest to those men? Putting everything we have in their care?" he asked her time and again.

From the first day of their trip, Isaiah was confident he had won her approval. He was the personification of her life, the fruit of her womb and she cherished him like a budding orchid needing only to be sheltered from the harsh light of the world to blossom into something splendid to behold.

"When you do return to the store, you must not think you can be your father all over again," she cautioned.

"And why not?"

"Because your father was a different man who lived in different times," Rosa replied.

"But his goal in life was to create a merchant son, so that his only child could carry on as president," Isaiah countered petulantly. "Only now Nathan Bloomberg has taken that position for himself and is preparing his son Jacob to fill it when he is gone. You must tell them that I am coming," he insisted.

The moment he made that speech, Isaiah was certain he had finally convinced Rosa that it was time for him to return to the store. Yet, being the mother of a pint-sized man-boy, she was unable to put aside her fears for her son. Isaiah was small, bordering on tiny for his age. And Rosa could do no more than merely nod her head in response to his demands, telling him they would talk, after the Christmas rush.

"We must wait until things settle down at the store," she said uncertainly. She was aware Isaiah had been buying thick-soled shoes and padded shoulders in his suits and overcoats, hoping to achieve the impossible with his tiny body. What only he seemed to appreciate was that there was a strong inheritance of Asa's image and reputation imbedded in his character, which gave him a stature impossible for others to ignore.

It was difficult for Rosa not to slip into a fantasy of her son replacing Asa, her husband. There were times when she felt almost immoral, casually accepting him as if she had known him intimately; with no modesty, nor reserve in their being together.

***

Regardless of his mother's concerns, Isaiah was not prepared to wait. While Rosa continued to urge him to wait for the right time for him to appear at the store, he got up early on his first morning home. Dressing quietly in his most formidable suit, he slipped into his father's closet to try on one of the grey homburgs that had become Asa's sartorial trademark. Fitting the hat over his center-parted, close-cropped wiry hair, he paused to review his reflection in the mirror. He frowned, drawing his black, bushy eyebrows together in an attempt to appear as formidable as his child-like face would permit. It was a practiced pose that would identify him for the next forty years.

He was out of the house before daybreak, bathed and dressed. It was raining when he surprised Alex, the driver, in the middle of his breakfast. The chauffeur was dressed in his jodhpurs and leather leggings. However, the upper portion of his body was covered only by the tops of a suit of long underwear.

Alex was tolerantly pleased at having the family home and he greeted Isaiah without mentioning the homburg or the frown with which Isaiah viewed him. "You are up early," he remarked casually.

Isaiah, fully dressed, was standing in the doorway of the chauffeur's kitchen above the garage.

"I need you to drive me to the store in the Packard," Isaiah announced.

"And how about your momma?" the chauffeur replied, trying to make the question sound innocent, while not quite sure of his ground.

"You are referring to Mrs. Wolfe?" Isaiah asked coldly.

"Why, yes," Alex admitted.

Four years abroad had changed Isaiah and Alex was struggling to adjust to his new relationship with the boy, uncertain of the extent of the lad's authority. Isaiah had planned on that, when he intentionally declined Alex's invitation to ride up front on the drive home from the railroad station. "Come sit up in front with me lad, so I can catch up on what you have been up to," the chauffeur had suggested, indicating the open door by the driver's seat. Isaiah had smiled a condescending smile and stepped into the rear seat beside his mother, leaving the door open for the driver to come around to close it behind him.

In the chill of the morning with the polished Packard silently waiting, the chauffeur again hesitated. His uncertainty was apparent to Isaiah's shrewd eye. Jobs were scarce, very scarce and Alex sensed that how he handled this could cost him his position. If not immediately, then in time as authority was passed on to the boy. There was very little sentiment in Isaiah Wolfe, just as there had been little in his father. Only complete obeisance and loyalty were what mattered. Both Asa and his son measured little else.

The chauffeur sensed that to challenge this pampered son, a boy he had paddled across his knees more than once, was a relationship that no longer existed. Yet he was uncomfortable, and instinctively reluctant to surrender the remaining vestige of his adult authority. "Surely you have time for a spot of tea, lad?"

"Alex. You are to drive me to the store, now. My mother is not to be awakened. And I expect to be at Wolfe & Bloomberg by eight thirty." It was the exact schedule that had been kept by Asa Wolfe in his last years, including the punctual arrival time at the employee entrance a half hour before opening. The significance of the boy's plans did not go unnoticed by the chauffeur.

"And Alex, if we are late, you can be sure it will not happen again because of my driver's inability to follow instructions." He went on to remind the chauffeur that the servants' day began at seven, the hour designated for Alex to be dressed and ready. Things had slackened off since Asa laid down the rules.

Isaiah turned away from the kitchen door and went to the side of the Packard, waiting for the middle-aged Scot to slip into his high-button driving jacket. Isaiah was comfortable in the knowledge of the power of his will and his position; having dressed in his new European clothes that aged him -- in his own mind -- far beyond his nineteen years.

The driver swiftly appeared fully dressed in tunic top and cap, but once again opened the car's front door. There was the beginning of a smile on the Scot's dour face that seemed to say, 'I'm-on-your-side, lad.' The front seat had been where Isaiah rode when driving to St. Georges School, or to horse riding sessions or on casual trips to the dentist office. Seated up front alongside each other, the chauffeur had adopted a form of ersatz paternalism. Only now Isaiah ignored the open door, waiting alongside the rear of the Packard for the driver to open the passenger door before stepping into the back seat.

Alex performed exactly as Isaiah planned, quietly taking up his place behind the wheel and starting the engine. Then, with a swift glance in the rearview mirror he was momentarily startled at the sight of Isaiah watching his every move from beneath the large grey homburg. The resolve in the boy's eyes, and the dark eyebrows over the bridge of his long nose combined to turn his thoughts back to memories of his silent obeisance to Asa Wolfe. Alex could feel the intensity of the boy's eyes on the back of his neck just as he had felt the eyes of Isaiah's father.

Twice he attempted to break the sense of subjugation while working the Packard through the morning traffic. "You haven't been down to the stable yet lad?"

When Isaiah was under his thumb, Alex would take Isaiah to the stables and supply him with cigarettes and look the other way when his young charge did things his father would not approve. Asa had always kept a stable of show horses, Tennessee Walkers and prize saddle breeds. With the corridors between the stalls carpeted with hemp rugs, the stables were a prime place for children's parties, the hay loft and corridors great places for hide and seek games.

"While you were away, Jake Bloomberg's kids have been dropping by a couple of times," Alex remarked, glancing into the rear view mirror. "They wanted to use the stables for a party, like the parties we once held there. I told them the place wasn't fit for parties anymore," Alex added, uncertain if his chatter was penetrating Isaiah's isolation. Isaiah remained quiet.

"I guess you plan on going to college after Christmas, eh, Laddie? Do you think you can stand our schools after a taste of those fancy European places?"

Still Isaiah didn't respond partly out of his determination to keep Alex in his place, but primarily because he was concentrating on what lay ahead. Alex heard, without turning his head, the sound of the glass rolling shut, sealing off the driver.

The fleet of dark blue company delivery vans had already claimed all the curbside space, making the side street to the store's loading dock impassable. Because of Asa's political connections, the big store had established proprietary rights to the entire side street, ignoring competitors' and public protests. The store was acting as if the street was part of the Wolfe & Bloomberg domain. Alex nosed the Packard carefully through the maze of trucks, the appearance of the big car bringing an almost electric stillness to the mass of moving dollies and freight carts.

As the now aging Packard approached the employee's entrance, the driver looked again into the rearview mirror. Isaiah met his eyes and didn't move. The car came to a full stop.

The employees who were filing into the store had stopped at the entrance to see who got out of the big car. Some of the old timers thought they were seeing a ghost with the figure in the back seat wearing the grey homburg. A truck pulled up behind the car and honked brashly. Alex twisted uneasily in his seat, then with a submissiveness made awkward by his delay, he stepped out of the car to hold open the passenger door. The thought passed through his mind that only few years ago, he had been a surrogate parent and disciplinarian to this squirt. He had never hesitated administering what he felt Isaiah lacked in his upbringing, with the tacit, though unspoken, approval from Rosa.

Over the years the chauffeur had become more than a driver for this family, as he was more than a servant to Rosa. His special place with the widow had won him many favors and much authority around the family estate. But Alex understood, with canny Scottish good sense, that all the goodwill on earth wouldn't last him five seconds in a confrontation with the slim figure stepping out of the car. Almost unconsciously, he touched the peak of his cap in obeisance as Isaiah stepped onto the pavement.

"Alex," Isaiah said quietly in impersonal tones, looking into the driver's ruddy face. "I expect we will be doing this again tomorrow and every day the store is in business from now on. And Alex, if you give me one more God damn performance like we have gone through this morning, I promise you will not only lose your job but you will remember for a long time the price you will pay for your God damn foolishness. Have I made myself clear?"

"Isaiah," the chauffeur stammered. But before he could utter his words of explanation or apology, his thoughts still taking shape in his state of shock, Isaiah interrupted.

"Pick me up at six thirty. And Alex, if I'm not here at the door, wait for me at the store garage."

Isaiah Wolfe momentarily closed his eyes as he passed through the employee entrance, past the time clock, into the store that morning. He was allowing the soft murmur of the huge store to come to him, each sound placing itself in his memory. There was the snap of the time clock on employee cards as they filed in for the day, the soft shuffling of feet across the open floors, the distant register bells and the subdued chatter coming through the corridors, mixed with the smells of wax and furniture oils and the fine scent of glass polish from freshly cleaned fixtures. It all formed a mystical cacophony, orchestrated like no other sound to Isaiah's ear. This wasn't his first day in the store. This was his return and he let it all come to him in a rush. The power of it made his body rise in his shoes to heights that made him momentarily dizzy as he nodded briefly to the 'good mornings' from those who stood aside and quietly watched his progress through to the main floor to the elevators.

These were his children, and he would see to them in their troubles and sickness, and he would bring them the leadership and security and supply the authority they sought. The bell sounded, alerting the last of the clerks to the moment they must appear in departments for inspection and sales instructions. Three minutes. Isaiah glanced up at the face of the iron filigreed clock above the main entrance when a voice spoke close to his ear.

"Good morning, Mister Wolfe, sir."

Isaiah wheeled, ready to challenge the reverence he imagined to be a note of sarcasm in the woman's voice that had added the "sir" to his name. He found himself facing a diminutive, green-eyed girl, the morning rain visible in her ginger colored hair. The thought passed through his mind that the rain was clinging to her like gentle tears. He was surprised to see the look of reverence in her eyes.

"It's good to have you in the store, to see you here this

morning," the girl said.

Isaiah was puzzled. He knew that voice from somewhere out of the past, but where? Perhaps it had come from someone in the tangled memory of his father's wedding? He was sure only that it was a voice he had heard as a boy. Yet he was certain he knew that face, though it was momentarily lost among the faces of a dozen different memories drifting about in and out, vignettes of another time. Yet he knew he had seen her somewhere, a little less tired, perhaps less harried, yet strangely familiar. The girl continued to avoid his recall.

The in-store bell began sounding again, a steady ringing heralding the opening of the customer doors at both the main store entrances.

"What's your name?" he asked. Then it came to him, as if the ringing of the opening bells had awakened his recall. "Desdemona Gonne." He blurted out the name before the girl could reply. "I remember you, the girl who hates to be called Patricia. We rode the Ferris wheel together. Do you work here in the store?" Isaiah asked, his voice rising above the bursts of noise.

But the girl was already moving into the main aisle beyond his voice, disappearing among the scurrying clerks. "Of course she does," he told himself. There was never any question in his mind that he would see her again. "But that can wait," he muttered to himself. "There are other things for you to be thinking about before you go chasing after her."

***

For years Asa Wolfe had watched the store opening from where his son now stood. The old man had waited, pocket watch in hand, for the bells' call to business. At the first sound he would announce in a modulated voice, speaking to himself and any standing close enough to hear. "We are now open for business." It was the exact phrase he had used on opening day in the spring of 1887, and every store opening since. In the temporary silence following the bells, Isaiah swore he could hear the voice of his father, even as he joined in repeating the words in unison.

Each day in the big store was to be a new record sales day for the late Asa Wolfe. His goal was to surpass the same day of a year ago, with bigger dollar volume, though not always larger profits. And when the clerks and the drivers made the goals he had set for them, Asa was delighted and warm, standing by the employee doors to shake their hands and wish them all good night. And when they failed, using the excuse of rain or snow or a scheduling of holidays, he was dour and unforgiving.

Record days, though less frequent, were still discussed in the Wolfe & Bloomberg board room, but only with department heads in executive session, no longer bantered about with the help as the founder had done.

The late Asa Wolfe would personally make it a point to appear in the department where the particular quota for the day was high; usually because of a special-sale advertising budget. Once there, he would write the target figure for the day on a slip of paper with his grease pencil. He would then post the paper on the cash registers in the department. Intermittently, throughout the day, he would reappear to lift the register shields to read the totals.

"Come on gentlemen," - or ladies as the case may often be. "We are going to make it. You are doing fine. Who is going to put this department over the top for me?" And the spirit, the game of making the sales target for Asa Wolfe, more often than not, carried the day.

Other times on opening hour, he would shout out an order across the floor of a department. "Gentlemen, or ladies in a women's' department, we have special opening prices for our early customers. Until ten o'clock, every item in ladies lingerie is twenty percent off the listed sales price." Another day it would be men's shoes or the entire ladies ready-to-wear department, discounted until ten. There was always some surprise, some incentive to get the store open with momentum and the crowds would push through the big brass-trimmed doors to hear the old man's pronouncement for the day.

The morning Isaiah came through the employees' door wearing his father's grey homburg, Wolfe & Bloomberg was no longer just one big store, there were branches in three states.

Asa hurried up the brass-trimmed marble staircase to the mezzanine to look across the block square expanse of the main floor of the anchor store. Feeding hungrily on the scene, he felt the presence of his father as he listened to the sounds of the pneumatic tubes whizzing over the aisles on all-but invisible wires, and watched the conveyor baskets flying back and forth; his heart pounding with the excitement. These sounds were the heartbeat, the pulse of the big store.

Isaiah started for the elevators as the center aisle began filling with wet shoppers, some rain-soaked with hats and umbrellas, having waited in the rain for the opening. They were hurrying in the excitement of the first moments of opening; ferreting through the morning price reductions. Isaiah, his thin shoulders drawn back to add height to his topcoat, stepped into the first elevator cage, nodding his acknowledgment to the customers pushing into the lift. He had forgotten his father's homburg on his head, assuming the second glances and curious stares were the result of customers recognizing him. In truth, the curious stares were coming from mothers startled to see a young boy wearing an old man's hat. Their stares were lost on Isaiah, his mind racing ahead to the sixth-floor corner office beyond the glass door where Asa had ruled the store.

He would soon discover that tiny office was no longer a part of the executive suite. Distant relatives of the Bloombergs, bent on establishing a position in the store with their name on the door and carpeted offices, had all but buried Asa' sixth-floor den at the end of the hall. His father had refused to refurbish or change anything, including the glass panel door which was always open. Following his death, Rosa let it be known nothing was to be disturbed.

"Hosiery, ladies ready-to-wear, linens, towels, housewares, hardware, radios and phonographs, records, men's wear, furniture, linens and yard goods." Each passing floor was announced by the slim, nervous elevator girl. Finally, Isaiah was alone in the car facing the fuzzy-haired operator. "Fifth floor. Cafeteria, imports, mail order and books," she repeated, waiting for him to step out.

"I'm going to the sixth floor," Isaiah said.

"But there is nothing on six except the general offices, the credit department and employment," she said. "And they don't open until nine thirty, sir."

"I am Isaiah Wolfe. Do you not think I have any business going to the executive floor?" He asked with the sarcasm that was to mark his appearance for years to come. "And might I ask, are you chewing gum?"

"Yes sir," the operator answered, immediately swallowing her gum as she pulled the doors shut and rolled the cage up to the top floor. "Good morning, Mister Wolfe," she said respectfully as he stepped out of the car. For the second time that morning Isaiah turned, unsure for the moment whether he had detected a deprecating note of ridicule in the operator's voice. He had only to glance back to see the girl had been startled after her first flippant reply. The importance of her job had her quickly trying to make amends. Isaiah smiled diffidently and stepped out into the world that had been controlled by his father for thirty years, a control now usurped by cousins and uncles wearing the crown Isaiah instinctively knew to be rightfully his.

Isaiah was counting on their underestimating who and what he represented, yet he was fully aware they would not easily relinquish their control. He could see it in their condescending smiles when they spotted him coming down the hall in his father's grey homburg, the picture of an adolescent, made vulnerable by his own preposterous posing. There wasn't among any of them the slightest recognition of the iron and shrewdness of the old man surging through his veins, dominating his every thought. They were equally slow to recognize that this was a fighter who fought without rules of honor and dignity, an unusually cold, impersonal fighter who would learn quicker and hate harder than any man they had known.

It was Nathan Bloomberg himself who first stepped out to face him. Having learned of Rosa's return to the city, Nathan had come in early in the event she would show up at the store unannounced. He now stood with his thumbs hooked triumphantly into his vest pockets, blocking Isaiah's progress. Rocking back on his heels and towering over the boy, he asked. "And to what do we owe the honor of this early visit?"

Isaiah looked up past the vast expanse of expensive flannel into the florid face of his father's cousin, a face that in Isaiah's eyes looked down on him like an arrogant cat hovering over a mouse. Nathan Bloomberg's loose, weak mouth spread in what was intended as a semblance of a smile.

"This visit?" Isaiah replied in a voice reflecting his puzzlement.

"Does your mother know you are here?" Nathan asked, with a note of paternal concern. There was an awkward pause before he added: "Or is she with you this morning?"

"Why do you ask? Do you have business with my mother?" Isaiah answered, falling into his father's trick of answering a question with a question.

Nathan's eldest son Jacob appeared at his father's side along with two other relatives Isaiah only vaguely recalled. The absurd grey hat resting on Isaiah's head and the recollection of the ridicule Jake had taken at the hands of the elder Wolfe inspired him with a moment of reckless courage.

"Well, the son returns," he announced with a smirk, recalling the years of Asa's insults. "It's time someone told you to go shit in your hat, Wolfe. But I suspect you have something more important do with that hat." He reached out and lifted the homburg from

Isaiah's head, a boy's playful trick.

"Asa Wolfe," he said, reading the printing in the hat band. "A Borsalino. You must have picked up the wrong hat, Isaiah. This hat belongs on a man's head." He flipped the hat in a sailing motion over the partition into Asa Wolfe's office where it landed precisely on the worn wooden desk.

There followed an immediate silence. The smile disappeared from the elder Bloomberg's face. Nathan was beginning to sense something of the presence of the late Asa Wolfe in this thin, diminutive shadow standing before him. He searched his mind for some authoritative rhetoric that would reestablish his place of command, but his mind was suddenly recalling the haunting fact that this sprout and his mother voted twenty-eight percent of the Wolfe & Bloomberg corporate stock. Those shares, which up until now had rested somewhat compliantly in Rosa's hands. Nathan struggled briefly trying to recall the rules of custodianship and Isaiah's age before forcing a smile.

"Welcome home, Isaiah. You know you are always welcome in the store. And please, don't let Jake's horses-ass schoolboy's antics upset you." Nathan Bloomberg smiled, stepping aside to make room for Isaiah's passage.

The rage surging through Isaiah's cheeks flared undisguised and visible for them all to see, as one by one they faded into the offices off the hall; each of them aware they had been contaminated by Jacob Bloomberg's monumental blunder. A few of the entourage, those who had attached themselves to Nathan Bloomberg's prominence, quickly detached from their alliance and followed Isaiah to the door to Asa's office. It was locked. Isaiah shook the handle then turned to scan the corridor for Nathan Bloomberg. He was gone. Those who had accompanied him stood motionless, unsure of the power they thought they had seen settling on the boy.

"Who has the key?" Isaiah snapped.

One of the cousins stepped forward. "Your mother keeps the

key to that office."

Isaiah silently cursed himself for being unprepared, aware that all eyes in the hall were now focused on him. Some had left their desks and were now watching the confrontation between the nineteen-year-old and the glass-paneled door. Isaiah considered wandering off through the store, though he knew instinctively this was a confrontation he must win.

Without hesitation, he crooked his arm, thrusting the elbow of his heavily coated sleeve through the glass in the door. "Have someone from maintenance see to that glass," he said quietly to no one in particular, then reached through the shattered window, to open the door from the inside handle. The noise brought a miraculous reappearance of Nathan Bloomberg.

"What in hell is going on here?" Bloomberg demanded charging toward Asa's office, before stopping as quickly as he had appeared. His glance down the hallway had caught sight of the ominous cloud of black satin and feathers that had suddenly appeared billowing down the corridor from the elevators.

CHAPTER 11: ISAIAH RETURNS

It took the better part of four years, seven days a week, of Isaiah's reviewing operating statements, balance sheets and examining invoices, warehouse receipts, inventory turnover and seasonal advertising budgets before he began to establish his voice in the affairs of Wolfe & Bloomberg. And though Nathan Bloomberg retained his title as chief executive at the head of the table – with his son Jake seated at his right – in what were largely make-believe board meetings, the making of decisions began to inextricably shift to Isaiah. He worked harder. Studied longer. And with the blood of his father pulsing through his every thought, he made himself the best merchant in the business.

It was during this transition that Isaiah first mentioned the possibility of Nathan's running for United States Senate. He did it subversively, seeding the idea with innocuous questions to Nathan's son Jacob, confident that his compliments and praises regarding Nathan's popularity would be repeated.

Jacob had never been able to accept the idea that Isaiah, not Jake, would take over the store once Nathan was out of the way.

It was during the third year of Isaiah's return to the big store that his future took its final step toward assuming full control of the company. He was deep into budgeting figures, measuring past sales with comparable ad budgets on various media outlets, when Nathan appeared in his open office doorway. Isaiah had established a reputation of being able to isolate his thinking to the point of absolute concentration. Until Nathan Bloomberg put one hand to his mouth and coughed politely, he never noticed his father's cousin standing in the doorway.

"Nathan. Damn, you startled me. But I'm glad you are here. I want to share some of these sales and marketing thoughts with you before —"

Nathan interrupted. "That's not what I came to discuss," he said, heavily dropping his large body into an office chair opposite Isaiah's desk. "I have a problem and you may be able to help. I certainly hope so, because word has it you are as excited about my running for senator as I am."

Isaiah pushed the mound of papers on his desk aside. "Whatever I can do, consider it done," he said briskly.

"I need money," the elder Bloomberg said bluntly. "A lot of money. I thought perhaps we could pay a special corporate dividend."

"Am I permitted to ask the reason?" Isaiah asked.

Bloomberg grunted his reply. "This happens to be a personal matter." Isaiah had picked up rumors of Bloomberg's running off to the eastern part of the state with his paramour of the moment, though he had dismissed the stories as merely one of the rumors growing out of the gubernatorial campaign.

"Is this a situation that you have under control?" Isaiah asked.

"It is, if I can get my hands on some quick cash," Bloomberg replied.

"How much?"

"Fifty thousand dollars."

"Shit. There is no way the company can pay that kind of a dividend and still maintain our pledged bank balances. We would violate our loan agreements. Nate, that's more money than you have raised for your entire campaign. Fifty thousand is a helluva lot of money." Isaiah pushed his chair back from the desk while shaking his head.

"The bitch has said if the money isn't coming her way, she's going to the papers with our story," Nathan sighed. He looked drawn, his sun-tanned complexion now an odd color resembling a corpse Isaiah had once viewed that was exactly that color. It was in a travelling desert museum display; supposedly the body of the Mexican General Pancho Villa.

"This bitch has even threatened me with a breach of promise suit, and I'm supposed to be a happily married man. Of course I don't dare go to the banks with this," Bloomberg shrugged. "I might just as well stand on the corner of Hastings and Granville and announce the affair to the whole damn state."

"Look, Isaiah. I know that you happen to vote a good chunk of the Bloomberg family stock. Let's say I give you my word that things will stay that way once I am elected. You go ahead and talk to the dame. Pay her off, and whatever it costs you, I will make it up to you, one way or another."

"Well it's obvious that you are the last person to be negotiating with some woman who has been licking your balls," Isaiah said, dropping one of the rumors he had picked up.

"Who told you that?" Bloomberg shot back.

Isaiah, unable to restrain a sarcastic smile, ignored the point of question. "I happen to have heard some of the details of this affair of yours," he replied. As he spoke, he was thinking of the seven bank accounts of each of his father's real estate companies that were now owned by his mother. The total balances in those accounts came close to the fifty thousand dollars.

"Suppose I go visit the lady and see if we are able to negotiate some way to keep her happy without the fifty thousand dollars."

The elder Bloomberg painfully pulled himself out of the chair and came around the desk. "Whatever the price, my promise holds," he said, reaching out to bury the little man in his chest. "You are everything your father hoped you would be," he said with passion. "Asa would be proud."

***

Perversely, Isaiah found himself enjoying the challenge of dealing with this out-gunned woman from the store's accounts payable department. His main hope was that she had not been talking to an attorney. Her name was Ellen Simpson, a tall, willowy, fifty-year-old blonde with shoulder-length hair, which she wore during office hours snuggly held in place by tight braids locked in a chignon. Since hooking up with Bloomberg, she had left the store's employ and when Isaiah traced her to a small but comfortable suit in the city's south hills, her hair was in full-flowing temptress mode.

Isaiah had called, introducing himself over the telephone and asking for a time when it would be convenient for him to drop by. Intrigued, the woman suggested any time. So that same afternoon, less than twenty-four hours following Nathan's call for help, he was at her door. His intended approach was to present himself as an inept, confused and astounded cousin on a mission of mercy for a fallen cousin. He would avoid the fact that Bloomberg had found himself in several similar, unfulfilled commitments.

What he also didn't reveal, once he was seated on a couch in what had obviously served as the lovers' suite, was that his briefcase held a documented release from any further litigation and a sworn denial that there had ever been any kind of a monetary settlement. These had been drawn up in absolute confidence by the corporate attorney, Abraham Rosenthal.

"There is no way that Nathan can come up with anything close to the money you are asking," Isaiah began, purposefully avoiding even the mention of fifty thousand dollars. "So what do you suggest? Should we talk in terms of what is possible and take this discussion out of the world of fantasy, or go on dreaming of revenge?"

Ellen's immediate response was forty thousand, causing Isaiah a burst of laughter.

"Good girl," he smiled. "I knew I was dealing with someone from accounting. Now let's be practical. He opened his briefcase and watched as the woman's face flushed with excitement at the sight of so much cash. "I have brought eight, no..." he fumbled through the briefcase as if needing to count the contents for the first time. “There is close to twelve thousand dollars in here. This is all Nathan could raise. I can tell you, this will leave him destitute. Losing you has utterly destroyed him and taken all the life out of the man.”

“He is still going to be senator, isn’t he?” the girl asked uncertainly.

“Who can predict what he will do now he has lost you,” Isaiah said sadly.

When the negotiations were complete and Ellen Simpson had signed her full name to the agreements, Isaiah stacked the eleven thousand in bundles on the coffee table and left, pausing only to shake the girl’s hand, a parting gesture to their agreement.

***

In the year Isaiah took tactical command of Wolfe & Bloomberg, the company had established a dozen branch stores generating annual sales of eight hundred million a year; it was a marketing power that commanded complete obeisance and compliance from manufacturers, suppliers and politicians. In the New York garment district, it had become common parlance to speak of the three markets out west as Los Angeles, San Francisco and Wolfe & Bloomberg.

CHAPTER 12: ROSA'S FALL

Rosa's drinking had become noticeable to Isaiah, long before his four years in the Austrian boys school. For a time, it was only apparent in the seclusion of their home. However, in Europe, she drank more openly, usually starting her day with wine for lunch, followed by afternoon cocktails.

Isaiah, burdened with the growing power that was shaping his future in the company, had little time to concern himself with his mother's drinking; until the night when she unintentionally let the air out of his soaring sense of self importance.

Mother and son were dressing for dinner in Rosa's bedroom suite in the Wolfe home; Isaiah busily re-tying his necktie for the third or fourth time, while Rosa was crowding the setting sun. "I never take a drink before sunset," she would proclaim, ignoring the mid-afternoon cocktails as if they had never passed her lips. She had already justified a few through the afternoon preparing for the chat she intended to have with her only child. She was sipping a gin cocktail when she decided the time was right to announce the surprise she had been preparing for her only son.

"I have been having lunch meetings with Abraham Rosenthal here at the house for the past several days," Rosa said. Isaiah noticed without a great deal of concern that her articulation was already slightly slurred. "Abe has presented me with a wonderful opportunity. He has come up with a proposal that insures you will never have to concern yourself with the Bloomberg family stock holdings in the firm."

"And how is that slippery bastard?" Isaiah asked, absently patting his neck tie in place.

"Are you not interested in what it is that Abraham and I have been discussing?" Rosa replied, offended by his lack of interest.

"Of course I am interested, Mother. I am interested in everything you do," he replied tolerantly.

"Remember, Abraham Rosenthal was your father's most trusted attorney."

"He didn't trust any of the lying bastards in that business," Isaiah replied.

"You forget, it was Abe who was trusted to deliver the cash for your father whenever Asa had dealings with political people," Rosa said defiantly. "And now he has come up with an opportunity to insure your role as the future chairman of the firm. I have decided he knows what he is doing."

Isaiah turned to face her, his antenna aroused. "And what is it that you have decided?"

"Abe has suggested that I merge the family properties into Wolfe & Bloomberg in exchange for additional stock in the firm. And after my thinking his suggestion over, and knowing of how the Bloomberg's resent your growing authority, I decided it was a good idea."

"You mean he wanted you to merge our suburban store properties in exchange for Wolfe & Bloomberg stock?" Isaiah demanded, his voice rising at the suggestion.

"Yes. And that's what I have done," she replied, with an unmistakably defensive tone that implied it was her decision alone to make.

"Are you telling me that you have traded all the suburban properties, which Asa bought and built, specifically to lease to the company? You know that Poppa built those properties as a means of keeping the Bloombergs from taking control," Isaiah shouted. He had been shouting at his mother lately, a trait developed as his confidence and independence continued to expand. "Don't you understand? My father built those stores and leased them to the company as his insurance policy and mine."

"You must understand why I have done this," Rosa replied, as she went to the bedroom bar for the remainder of her gin. "It is the only way to assure that you will take over the company when Nathan is gone. It gives you thirty-two percent of the company stock. With thirty-two percent, Abe pointed out, there would be little chance for a sale or a merger."

"Nathan is already gone," Isaiah hollered. "He is never in the store. He is campaigning for his election as senator. And I suspect he will be elected. Mother. Mother. Mother," Isaiah wailed. "Why can't you understand? The reason Poppa bought that land and built those stores was so the Bloombergs would never dare remove him or me from the company. As long as we owned those centers, our family was secure. We made very appealing leases for each of those centers that are extremely profitable for Wolfe & Bloomberg. All we have ever charged amounted to a modest depreciation and property taxes. Those centers would be unobtainable today if father had not built them to insure his control"

"I don't care," Rosa sniffed defiantly. "With thirty-two percent of the stock, nobody is going to try to remove you from inheriting your rightful place. It had to be done," she insisted, a little less positively.

"Thirty two percent? You must have forgotten that there are some three hundred thousand shares, or eight percent of that thirty-two percent, that are owned by the Bloomberg cousins?" Isaiah said, his voice heavy with sarcastic bitterness. "Asa held the voting rights for that stock as long as he was alive, because he knew how to manage the company and he owned the key properties. Now that you have sold the properties, we no longer have their assurance that the stock will remain in our hands. What kind of a deal did you make for the properties?" Isaiah demanded.

"Abraham said the only way the Bloombergs would entertain the idea was if we priced the properties for what they were worth. He said the exchange would have to be at the book value. It was the only way it could be done without what Abe called a substantial conflict of interest." She shrugged. "So we did the exchange at the book value."

“You took it upon yourself to give away the family properties, at a depreciated book value, in exchange for less than six percent of the firm stock?” Isaiah was dumbstruck. “Mother. A decent percentage rent for those properties would have made the book value five or ten times the stated book value.”

“I don’t care,” Rosa replied. “I could not stand by and see you sucking up to young Jacob Bloomberg like he was about to become president of Wolfe & Bloomberg. Furthermore, I do not appreciate you raising your voice to your mother, who has only your interest at heart,” she shouted right back at him.

They continued hollering at one another until Rosa, her gin glass tilting precariously in one hand, started for the stairway. “Anyway. I’m going down for dinner,” she announced, starting out the bedroom door. “You have already spoiled my gift to you.”

***

Asa built the Wolfe Estate to serve as his lure in his campaign of convincing Rosa Lintel into marrying him. They had their first disagreement over the sweeping staircase that flows down into the majestic open hallway. Asa argued against incorporating a curved stairway.

“Steps on a curving stairwell are never the same width,” he argued. “Depending on the curve, the steps are broad at one end and narrow on the other. People are accustomed to steps always being the same width. When you shorten one end of the step and expand the other, people will fall. It’s just too damn dangerous. That’s the reason I never allow curved steps or steps of different heights in the stores. From the days people first learn to walk, they are unconsciously trained to steps being of a standard size and depth.”

However, Rosa insisted on a sweeping staircase. In her romantic moments, she dreamt of one day having a daughter coming down the stairs with her gown flowing in her wake, and a man waiting breathlessly at the foot of the stairs. Perhaps Rosa had even imagined herself in that role.

Her fall started at the first curve, the third step in the stairway. She was reaching for the railing when her ankle turned on the short step. She went down, turning and twisting over thirty-eight steps, finally coming to rest at the foot of the stairs. Her body, disjointed and bruised, landed beneath the table where she had watched the undertakers wash the naked remains of her husband. She continued to lie there; Isaiah was totally unaware she had fallen until the cry of a serving maid some ten minutes later brought him running down the stairs.

CHAPTER 13: ABRAHAM ROSENTHAL

Abe Rosenthal's top-heavy body moved with surprising agility the moment he spotted Isaiah stepping out of the Wolfe family Packard. The rotund, constantly sweating attorney beat the car's chauffeur to the rear car door, flinging it open with his ingratiating smile, so much a part of his sycophantic personality.

"I have been waiting here for you all morning," he said, mockingly scolding before Isaiah had a chance to step out of the car. "You are late. What happened to that reputation of yours for showing up thirty minutes before the store opening bell? Look, I have some really great news to share with you. It will take me twenty minutes in your office to lay out the details. Your mother and I put the finishing touches together yesterday on a wonderful deal, just for you. I guarantee, you won't be sorry if you can give me twenty minutes of your time."

Isaiah, still simmering from a sleepless night, during which he rode in the ambulance with his mother to the General Hospital, had already made up his mind to challenge Rosa's sale of the family-owned shopping centers. He was about to brush the fawning attorney aside, until he experienced a mystical transformation, a trait which was to become a part of Isaiah's character and management style. It was as if his father's spirit had whispered in his ear.

'The damage has already been done. There is no point in telling this shyster of your mother's fall or of having admitted her to the hospital under an assumed name to avoid the press. And you do know your chances of undoing Rosa's signature on the agreement are all but nonexistent. Swearing at this sonofabitch will make you feel good. But then you lose the bastard forever.'

Instead, Isaiah smiled.

“Good morning, Abe. Rosa gave me some of the details last night at dinner. Come on up to the office where we can talk.”

In the meeting that followed that morning, while leaving a lot unsaid with details to be worked out over time, Isaiah felt like a mongoose dodging a fat poisonous snake. It became immediately apparent that Abe Rosenthal was primarily interested in cementing his future with the big store, and if it happened to be in the cards, he would like to one day be named to the State Supreme Court.

He left the meeting assured of Isaiah’s need for him, departing with his assurance that the Bloomberg cousins stock would remain “in the bag.” Like Isaiah, the Bloomberg cousins’ were aware that Nathan Bloomberg was planning on leaving the store for the world of politics. And as Nathan’s son Jacob, was no match for Isaiah at running the business, the door would open for Isaiah to step in as Chief Executive Officer. That is, with Abe Rosenthal’s counsel, of course.

The fact that Rosenthal had surreptitiously cleared the merger with Nathan Bloomberg, and had met seditiously with an inebriated Rosa to consummate the deal, convinced Isaiah of the attorney’s treachery. And from that morning on, whenever Rosenthal appeared in the store, usually for lunch, Isaiah never let the lawyer out of his sight. The impression that the two were inseparable friends was visibly apparent to anyone with an interest in the store.

CHAPTER 14: ALCOHOL REHABILITATION

The admitting doctor in the General Hospital Emergency Room, a thin-faced, tight-lipped trauma physician who had recently completed his internship at Johns Hopkins Hospital in Baltimore, was too busy tending to Rosa to make much of an obeisance to Isaiah's sense of self importance. The doctor appeared to be totally unimpressed with the diminutive relative fussing over the now mumbling form of the middle-aged woman on the gurney. He dismissed as irrelevant Isaiah's explanation of her falling down thirty-odd stairs, as well as his attempt to pass off her inebriation as simply a mild case of excessive celebration during a family reunion.

Isaiah had instructed the ambulance driver that their patient was a Mrs. Thelma Wallingford, a cousin, staying with the Wolfe family. It was his intention to maintain that pseudo patient name for the duration of her hospital stay. That required a fifty dollar gratuity to each of the two-man ambulance crew before he was convinced they would remember their instructions.

As a further result of this subterfuge, Isaiah, who was one of the hospital's lead donors, found himself sitting on a hard, oak bench in the waiting room. The doctor from Baltimore had failed to recognize him as the scion of Wolfe & Bloomberg. What made matters even more humiliating was that he was surrounded on the bench by ailing old men and women — most of whom, he surmised, already had outlived their usefulness and had one foot planted in their grave – as well as several wailing babies.

When it came time for the doctor to report on the condition of his patient to the apparent next of kin, he wasted little time or courtesy on bedside manners.

"She has been badly banged up," the physician said, his

surgical mask dangling beneath his chin, testimony to the man's recent struggle with the bruised and battered patient. "We took care of most of the lacerations. "You do realize that your relative is dead drunk. She must have been so damn drunk when she fell, her spine was like wet string. A fall like that could easily have broken her neck or worse. It could have killed her. How long has she been drinking like this?"

"As long as I can remember," Isaiah replied, suddenly eager for medical counsel. "Though lately her drinking has gotten a lot worse. She called me at the office early yesterday hollering that there were book worms coming out of the pages of the book she was reading."

For a passing moment the trauma doctor raised his eyebrows with a hint of a startled smile. "That must have been a helluva book," he muttered. "You ever think of admitting her to the hospital's alcohol rehabilitation ward?"

"No. But if you think that would help, couldn't you order her treatment?"

The doctor nodded, measuring this tiny man who was obviously worried about the large, drunken woman.

"What's your relationship to the patient?"

"I'm her cousin. I am prepared take care of all the costs, if that is a concern," Isaiah answered.

"And who is her regular doctor," the trauma physician asked.

"She's never seen anybody on a regular basis. Usually it's just for headaches or woman problems. That leaves it pretty much up to you, doesn't it?"

The doctor stroked his chin pensively. "I can admit her for a couple of days. That will give her time to get rid of the book worms. You will have to settle with the admitting office as to how long she'll stay. It will be up to you if she is admitted for the full rehabilitation program," he said. "They have specialists who know how to handle the drying out problems that lady is going to be dealing with."

That night, Rosa was admitted to the General Hospital alcohol rehabilitation program as Mrs. Thelma Wallingford. Her cousin, Isaiah Wolfe, paid the six hundred dollars advance payment.

***

To all appearances, Rosa surprised Isaiah in the manner in which she accepted his committing her to the ward for alcoholics. Perhaps, he reasoned, it must be something to do with the drugs they were administering to help her through her withdrawal.

Arriving at her room the following afternoon, his arms wrapped around a massive bundle of gladiolas, he discovered his mother sitting up in an easy chair. The only visible indication that she was in a hospital was the institutional blanket over her knees. She smiled a tolerant smile and asked whimsically. "Who in hell is this Mrs. Thelma Wallingford?"

"That happens to be you, for now," Isaiah replied. "You can go back to being Mrs. Asa Wolfe when it's time to go home."

"These people have been very nice to me, much nicer than you treat your own mother," she replied petulantly. "I think I will stay awhile. I'm not in much of a hurry to go anywhere," she said. "Besides, I seem to recall you were none too happy over my business dealings with Abe Rosenthal."

"That's all been taken care of," Isaiah assured her. "You know I have never trusted the sonofabitch and I still don't. But I have convinced him that I am his ticket to the State Supreme Court and to his holding a seat on the Wolfe & Bloomberg board of directors. So long as we keep an eye on him, things should be in order.

"I don't suppose honest Abe Rosenthal ever mentioned to you that he ran that whole property merger deal past Nathan Bloomberg before he ever brought it to you?" Isaiah added, making his point that she was to never trust the bastard.

Rosa revealed her surprise by uttering: "That slippery crook."

"I thought not," Isaiah added.

This caused his mother to fidget in her chair, eager to change the subject. "I had a visitor this afternoon," she announced. "It was a young man. He reminded me of you when you were young, and not so damn ambitious."

"A visitor? They are not supposed to allow anyone in this ward unless their names are on a list of family members," Isaiah replied testily. "I left instructions there were to be no visitors. We don't need the newspapers nosing into our family problems."

"So now I am a problem?" Rosa said.

"You are a constant problem," he smiled. "That is why Poppa courted you for as long as he did."

"Well, you should know that my young visitor happens to be a patient, so don't you go raising hell with the hospital staff," Rosa replied calmly. "There are quite a number of young people here with problems like mine. I like this boy. What's more, I am beginning to think I can be of help to him, and some of the others as well. Besides, it's good to have someone who listens to what I have to say for a change. This boy never had a mother. He has an older sister. She was the only mother he ever knew."

A nurse came in and took the flowers from Isaiah's arms and returned a few minutes later with the arrangement in a tall vase.

"It's not good for you to be sitting up too long on your first day here," the nurse scolded Rosa, indirectly sending a message to Isaiah that it was time for him to leave.

Isaiah, quick to pick up the suggestion, leaned over and kissed his mother's forehead. "I have to get back to the store. You do have a telephone? Use it to call me with whatever you need and I'll be back tomorrow." He nodded to the nurse, acknowledging her suggestion, and left.

"I don't need anything," Rosa said quietly, long after her son and the nurse had left the room.

It was during Rosa's stay in the alcoholic rehabilitation ward that year that Nathan was defeated in his run for senator and Isaiah was named chief executive officer and chairman of Wolfe & Bloomberg.

Nathan never recovered from his defeat at the polls. People close to him claimed he never made the effort. Nathan could never reconcile the voting public turning against him with his own concept of what he was offering them when he threw his hat in the ring. His loss was not only a blow to his inflated ego as much as it was a rejection of everything he valued in life.

The man who defeated him was a farmer from the eastern half of the state who grew wheat and raised cattle, who had served in the state legislature without accomplishment. The farmer appeared at campaign stops wearing jeans made by Levi Strauss and he gave interviews to the press from his farmhouse verandah, where he and his wife slept in a hammock during the hot summer months. He was a contradiction to everything Nathan held to be important.

Nathan withdrew from public life, gifted the family home -- where he had lived alone since the death of his wife -- to a community college and ultimately found his way back to Ellen Simpson. He died a few years after his defeat, leaving the bulk of his estate and his shares in the company in trust for Jacob, his only son, and Jacob's heirs.

***

Exercising his new authority as chief executive officer, Isaiah wasted no time signing the architecture assignments for the construction of three additional floors to the big store, and what were to be the longest flights of department store escalators north of Los Angeles.

CHAPTER 15: DESDEMONA REAPPEARS

Ten years had passed since the morning of Isaiah's eventful return to the big store. Tucked away on the back roads of his mind, though submerged in his struggle to the top, there lingered the memory of his first hectic morning and the chance meeting with the girl on the Ferris wheel. Though he had promised himself he would find her again, his concentration had been totally focused on establishing his inherited role at Wolfe & Bloomberg. That alone had all but erased his memory of Desdemona Gonne. Fate had a different plan.

***

The General Hospital rehabilitation program was partially patterned after the Alcoholics Anonymous handbook. In addition to medication, the treatment included sessions where the group of ten or twelve recovering alcoholics at various stages of recovery, stood to introduce themselves with the acknowledgment: "I am an alcoholic." Rosa was one of the first to stand before the class and had difficulty with the acknowledgment, even when using her assumed name, though finding it considerably less stressful using her alias. Which she did, escaping the indictment of herself when it came time to announce: "I am Thelma Wallingford, and I am an alcoholic."

Rosa, once sober and alert, was quick to recognize the familiar and unusual name when Andrew Gonne rose, introducing himself as an alcoholic. While the lingering effects of her tumbling down the Wolfe mansion stairs had clouded her recall of what happened that particular night, the name Gonne had been posted in her memory as a red flag of danger since the day she "rescued" her only son from that damn Ferris wheel. Isaiah's reluctance in revealing the girl's name during their drive to the beach, and his subsequent denial of any lingering interest, had only served as further warning to a mother of but one Jewish son with an interest in an Irish Catholic girl. Besides it being a most unusual name, Rosa had since traced the name Gonne to a lady named Maud, William Butler Yeats' apparently unrequited love.

While Rosa was uncertain how her newfound young friend could be used in dealing with her own arrogant child, she sensed that to know the young man would someday prove valuable. She chose the chair next to the young man, establishing a friendship that carried through the afternoon and well beyond.

Two days passed before Dessie Gonne had the freedom from her part-time job to visit her brother. When she arrived at the clinic directly from work she was told at the desk the patients were attending an evening therapy class. The nurse explained her brother would be free no earlier than seven o'clock.

Taking a seat in the waiting room, Dessie became deeply engrossed in the medical magazine outlining the stages and difficulties facing those seeking alcoholic rehabilitation. She was so deeply absorbed in the magazine that, when Isaiah Wolfe sat down in the chair beside her, she never looked up.

"Hi," Isaiah said.

Isaiah had never greeted anyone with 'Hi.' He was uncomfortable with that degree of familiarity, nor had he allowed himself to become friends with anyone at that level.

Sensing the presence of someone in the seat next to her, Dessie looked up. "It's you!" she exclaimed.

"You do remember me?" he said, immediately pleased to learn she had not forgotten. "We met at the street fair. We rode that broken down Ferris wheel together," Isaiah said, confident she too was remembering. "What's that you are reading?"

There were no introductions, no hints of sexual attraction; their meeting would best be described as two old friends discovering one another in an unexpected situation. It was as if they had bumped into one another on a bus.

"Hi," Dessie replied. "Of course I remember. You were so worried that day that we were not going to make it down to the ground," she said teasingly.

"Oh, I knew we were going to make it back to the ground. I just didn't know how it would happen," he said, his smile raising his eyebrows in a manner indicating he was enjoying the memory. From the time of their first meeting, Dessie had often thought about Isaiah, suspecting that he almost never smiled.

"And?" she said, indicating the magazine. "It's a story about the problem my brother Andrew is dealing with. He is an alcoholic. I guess I should say he is a recovering alcoholic now that he is a patient here. It's good to see you again, even if this isn't the kind of place you expect to find a friend."

Dessie was aware that she was feeling much better about meeting Isaiah than she had been in her meeting with Patrick Higgins. There were none of the guarded feelings she had in her meeting the lawyer and asking for his help with Andrew. She reasoned the difference may well have been the physical contrast in the two men. Isaiah was five foot four, maybe five five in his elevated shoes. His black bushy eyebrows met above his rather large nose. He was a little man, maybe weighing a hundred-and-thirty-five pounds. She had wanted to take him into her arms and protect him from the moment she first reached out and took his hand.

Higgins was at least a foot taller with the build of a wrestler. His penetrating brown eyes and quick, easy smile she recognized as his technique for winning a person's confidence, or perhaps putting a witness off guard.

"What brings you here?" Dessie asked innocently.

"It's a family thing, with me," Isaiah replied. "I have a relative in the program. The desk nurse told me they are in a meeting. Have you had supper?"

"I came straight from work," Dessie admitted.

"I did too. If you like, we can go someplace and eat when this therapy session is over. I have no idea how long it runs, but I'll wait for you here."

Isaiah was excited running into Desdemona Patricia Gonne; and while he was aware of being evasive, it was not because of any embarrassment that his mother was also in treatment. He was feeling his way in a new relationships and unsure of how far he should go. He was thinking of the destiny involved in his discovering this girl in a place where they each had someone needing help. The thought even entered his head that one day he may marry this girl and perhaps that is why he was being evasive, having heard that alcoholism runs in the family. He had already noticed she was not particularly attractive; physically, she was a little heavy in the hips, reflecting her Celtic breeding. Her hair, which obviously had a mind to do pretty much as it pleased, would, in all likelihood, resemble a rust colored mop when she awoke in the mornings. It was only after Dessie put the combs and brushes to her hair that the color would glow, moving in tune with her every move.

While Dessie lingered awhile with her brother, Isaiah sat waiting for her, having rushed through his visit with Rosa. She discovered him seated on the edge of a hard bench, despite the fact he was infamous around the store in his refusal to wait for anyone. After leaving the hospital, they shared a hamburger sitting at the counter in an all-night diner. Isaiah was driving his own car, in which he had a two-way radio to the store. He took pride in showing her how he could call the night security desk at Wolfe & Bloomberg and they would patch him into a telephone call.

"I can talk to New York with that," he boasted proudly. "And that's important when our goods don't arrive on time. I can give them hell from the car while I'm driving to the store. It's three hours later in New York," he explained.

"I work there too," Dessie said. "It's only part time. I have been on part time for years now, though my supervisor has been promising me there will be a full-time opening one day soon. I'm patient," she smiled. "Like you. That was nice, you waiting for me while I talked to my brother."

"I can take care of that part-time business," Isaiah offered quickly.

"No. Please don't. I know you are connected with the Wolfe family. That would mark me as somebody special. It could make things difficult for me, and I need the work."

"Connected with the family? Don't you know who I am? I am Isaiah Wolfe. I am the son of Asa Wolfe, the man who founded the store nearly five decades ago," Isaiah boasted.

Immediately he was wishing he could undo the boast. He had used the phrase 'I am' so many times that it came from his mouth as a matter of rote, a prepared and rehearsed speech. And she already knew who he was. What he saw in Dessie's face was a smile bordering on sympathy. He had hoped for something else, though unsure of what it was he expected.

"Whatever you say," Isaiah shrugged. If anyone at the store had suggested he back off doing a favor for a friend, he would have simply bullied his way with personnel and got her the full-time job.

It was becoming obvious to him that something about this girl was different; he saw it in the way she looked at him with his boasting. Whatever it was, he knew she was bringing about a change in his thinking. He experienced the same feeling the day she reached out to take his hand leading him onto the Ferris wheel. He recalled reaching out for the security of her hand when he was afraid they were about to be dumped out of that worn-out Ferris wheel. Dessie told him to look out at the ocean, to concentrate on letting his thoughts go beyond the horizon. She had taken his hand, sensing he was nervous in the loosely swinging Ferris wheel seat.

Isaiah was hoping she would do it again. And she had asked him – no, she had pleaded with him -- not to use his position in the store to win her a permanent job. 'She just makes so damn much sense,' He told himself.

Whatever change Dessie Gonne was bringing about in Isaiah, he quickly resolved it wouldn't make any difference in the way he would run the store. Nor would it make him any less cautious in dealing with the Bloombergs and Abe Rosenthal.

Desdemona Patrician Gonne landed her full-time job in a matter of weeks and then asked Isaiah to never speak to her while they were in the store.

She was clerking at the candy counter on the main floor where she had worked during busy seasons for years. Her first morning on the job full-time, Isaiah pretended to discover her there, though he dared not mention, and warned the personnel manager to never let on, that he had interfered with her being hired, afraid of what she might do if she were to learn of his role. Dessie continued to busy herself with the chocolate displays, pretending not to notice the company's top executive inspecting the confections counter.

Each of them became careful to never leave the store at the same time, though Isaiah was often involved in meetings that ran into the late hours. When that happened, he would call her from his car on the store-telephone-relay hook up, until Dessie learned what he was doing and scolded him harshly. That too was a new experience for the scion of the Wolfe family. When he could no longer call, he began appearing at the Gonne home late in the evenings and together they would go to eat in the roadside diner where they felt comfortable and unobserved.

Not once, in all the nights when they sat in his car and talked, sometimes until daylight chased him home, did Isaiah ever have so much as a passing thought about taking her to bed. He had found a friend, a friend so important to his being, that he never allowed the thought to enter his head. He needed to talk about the store, to talk about the Bloombergs and their cousins, especially those whose proxy-power he relied on to remain on top. He talked of his distrust of Abe Rosenthal, and about his father and how as a child he hated sitting on Asa's lap and lying to him; and how he felt uncomfortable whenever he sensed the old man's excitement rising on his warm buttocks whenever he invented an erotic scene to please him.

Dessie talked about her church, how at one time she had planned to take her vows; the idea had left her the day she noticed the long grey hairs growing from Sister Mary Hildegard's nostrils. "I don't know why that turned me off," she confessed. "I guess I always thought the nuns were so close to God. But the hairs in her nose," she shrugged, still baffled by her turn-off, "they were grey." She talked about her drunken stepfather, Seamus Ryan, who was not really a stepfather at all, but had been her mother's lover after the death of her husband. Ryan had not appeared at the Gonne home since Andrew's bout with the law. And she spoke of what she remembered of her father, the late Sergeant Major Harry Gonne, who had run the house like a battalion drill, lining Dessie up in the morning for room inspections.

"The worst thing that ever happened to Andrew was that his father died before the Sergeant Major had a chance to straighten him out," Dessie recalled, shaking her ginger curls. "He certainly straightened me out."

CHAPTER 16: ROSA RETURNS HOME

Rosa Wolfe was never the same following her stay in the General Alcoholic Program. She was notified she would be released following her ten days of treatment, though she was refusing to go. It was the first time she had been cold sober in years, and like her son, she was convinced she had discovered a new purpose in life. Rosa took an active interest in listening to the convoluted lives the young people revealed on their road to becoming alcoholics. She became a listener, a counselor, lending her candid experience to those who came to her room in the evenings needing to talk. When it came time for her release, she was irate and telephoned her son.

"Isaiah," she said, "you obviously don't need me anymore; you made that abundantly clear following my dealings with Abe Rosenthal. But I am needed here with these young people. And I intend to stay with them awhile. You can get by without my meddling in your affairs, so please, use your influence to see to it that I am allowed to stay."

Isaiah was startled. "That sounds fine with me, what does the hospital say?"

"That's why I'm calling you. They want me to go home. They claim my time here is up. They say they have done what they can; now it's up to me. That's pure bullshit. The staff just doesn't want me here helping these kids. It messes up their program. You wouldn't believe how many times these kids come to me for help, the kind of help only a recovering alcoholic can give them."

"So now you are admitting you are an alcoholic?" Isaiah replied.

"Of course, dear boy. What do you think they have been drilling into my head for the past ten days?"

Despite Isaiah's history as a major giver to all the city hospitals, he was unable to convince the doctors in the hospital's alcoholic ward to extend his mother's stay. What Rosa had intentionally overlooked in her call was that Andrew Gonne was being admitted to an extended-care program and, as he had become her surrogate son, she had taken his recovery under her wing. However, the hospital remained adamant and within days Rosa was back in the Wolfe mansion resuming her afternoon cocktails.

CHAPTER 17: FIRST SIGN OF TROUBLE

It was Dessie who made the move on Isaiah; as it was entirely driven by instinct, she never stopped to think what she was doing until it was too late. They had never so much as kissed or hugged one another. She had simply decided she wanted his child; nothing else would do. The minute she first laid eyes on Isaiah, she had fantasized having a baby seeded in her by this little man. His limousine, his mother and the fact he was the Wolfe of Wolfe & Bloomberg had made that appear out of reach, until things changed.

Seldom did a day pass that he wasn't at her door, or they were sharing a late night dinner. Isaiah had taken to staying late at the Gonne house. Always reluctant to leave, he had often been chased home by the early morning light.

In the beginning Dessie never realized she was trying to seduce him. Time and again she was startled to discover her hand on his thigh, always quickly taking it away before he noticed or seemed to. Then there were the deep, star-struck sighs and her gazing at him in a fashion that would have stirred the mating instincts of almost any man. When that failed, she began toying with his hair, twisting the tight curls on his neck around her fingers.

Late one night when the chemistry in her body took over, Dessie knew that she was ready. She was no longer aware nor did she care that she had been possessed by that instinct which motivates some women at that time of the month.

They were seated on the couch in the Gonne home, Isaiah explaining his problems in dealing with his mother's young cousin who had taken over and was now running the Lintel family millinery business. "I don't know how much I can steer his way, the goods are just not ..." Dessie stopped his story, putting her fingers to his lips. “I want you in me,” she whispered.

For an instant, Isaiah looked confused. “Now? Here? What if your brother…” Again she put her fingers to his lips.

“Now. I need to feel you inside me.”

“But I don’t have any…”

She merely put the tips of her fingers to his lips again, stood up, and, taking him by the hand, led him into the bedroom where she began unbuttoning his shirt.

“I can do that,” he said awkwardly.

Dessie stepped out of her underpants and lay back on the bed, raising her skirt above her hips, her eyes closed in expectation. “I have never done this,” she whispered from somewhere beyond her closed eyes.

Looking at her sturdy thighs, her legs parted at the ginger pubic hairs, Isaiah felt a flush of embarrassment at the erection suddenly visible through his trousers. Quickly, he stepped free of his pants and shorts and came down on top of her. “Be gentle,” she pleaded, taking him in her hand to guide his fumbling.

In the instant he was in her, it was over. Isaiah’s ejaculation lasted about as long as his initial thrust, though they continued to cling to each other while the last of what he had to give pulsed from his body into hers. “God. It is hot inside of you,” he muttered.

“Don’t come out, just yet,” she pleaded, holding him in the desperate grip of her legs and arms. They remained coupled until he felt her arms relax and he rolled free.

“I hope that doesn’t change things,” he said. “Between you and me, I mean.”

Dessie felt a glow of warmth flood over her. Facing him on the bed, she smiled. “I promise,” she said simply, her fingers teasing his bushy black eyebrows.

“I know I was too quick. But I couldn’t help it. It just happened. If we do it again, I will do it better.”

“I know,” she answered. “I’m hungry. You think you can afford to buy me a hamburger?”

“With onions?” He smiled.

They did it again, several times. Sometimes in Isaiah’s car with Dessie straddling him in the front seat; once in a stall at the Wolfe family stables on a bed of old straw. Isaiah had taken her there to show her the stables and the Wolfe estate. The straw made her sneeze violently while he was in her, causing Isaiah to believe he was finally doing it the way Dessie told him. And they did it again a month later, when she felt it was her time, though Isaiah was never a part of her planning. This time it happened.

Dessie Gonne discovered she was pregnant six weeks later; the subtle swelling in her abdomen bringing a broad smile to her face. It was only after the initial thrill had passed that she began to awaken to the consequences of what she had wished for. Slowly she realized that she had been possessed by an impossible dream. It took the irrefutable swelling of her body each day to overrule the fantasies of having a child with Isaiah. As the consequences of what she had done and the problems she faced continued to become more apparent each passing day, Dessie panicked.

She had no money. The house was held in trust for her and her brother. There was no way she could confess to Isaiah what she had done nor could she explain why. The physical urgency to complete the coupling, which had been so compelling for the past two months, was now only a vanished memory. To abort her pregnancy would condemn her soul for having committed the murder of her own child. There was only one way to face what she had brought upon herself; one person to whom she could turn.

CHAPTER 18: A SOLUTION

Sister Francis Clare, the swarthy complexioned Nun, whom Dessie always had thought of as Mexican or Latin American descent, was in truth the oldest daughter of an Italian immigrant millworker; a machine operator at the Dornbecher furniture factory. Joseph Bianco – who enjoyed the joke when someone who understood Italian called him Joe White -- had six sons before his Sicilian-born wife presented him with two girls: the first, Sister Francis, whose christian name was Elena; and then her younger sister, Genevieve Marie.

The day Dessie appeared at her classroom door, Sister Francis Clare was instantly alert to the possibility that something was troubling the woman she had known as a child. It had been several years since her matriculation, and while the nun had hoped Dessie would go on to college, she understood and accepted the limiting circumstances facing Dessie at home.

Over her years at Our Lady of Perpetual Help, many of the girls from her graduating classes had returned to Sister Francis to talk through the problems they faced in the outside world. The late thirties, were when young women entering the world from high school were ill prepared for the changes awaiting them in a world that was still a man's world.

Sister Francis was unable to recall how long it had been since she last saw Dessie Gonne; it must have been four years at least, maybe five. With so many passing faces of so many young girls, the teaching nun lost track of the students and the years. But Dessie she remembered. Dessie had been Sister Francis' star pupil.

The last class of the afternoon had been dismissed and the nun was at her desk marking class papers before leaving for vespers when she looked up and saw Dessie standing in her classroom doorway.

"Dessie Gonne," the nun declared with undisguised delight. "Come in, Dessie. Close the door and come sit here by my desk so we can talk," she said.

Dessie, wearing her black clerking dress with the lace collar, which the store encouraged women clerks to wear, took a deep breath as she sat facing the nun across the desk. "Sister, I am in trouble," she said quietly.

"Aren't we all," the nun replied, smiling while shaking her head wearily. "Just look at these papers. They are from my graduating class. It's more like the work of a class of third graders." She nodded her head wisely. "We don't see many students like you these days, Dessie." She reached across the desk and took the girl's hands reassuringly. "You know how happy I am to see you. You have always been one of the few bright moments in my work here at the school. Now why don't you tell me what it is that's bothering you? That's why you have come, isn't it?"

Again, Dessie inhaled a deep breath. "I'm pregnant," she said quietly. For an instant, she saw the disappointment reflected in the nun's weary face, and then it passed with a sad, slow nodding of her shrouded head.

"And not married," the nun said, finishing the unspoken sentence. "How long have you known this?"

"A month. Maybe two," Dessie replied. "I'm not sure."

The nun spoke hesitatingly, as if she were unable to get the words past her lips. "You mean -- this has been -- an on-going affair -- you have been carrying on?"

"More or less," Dessie whispered. "The first time was two months ago. But nothing happened then."

"And what about the man? What does he have to say about this?"

"There is no way I can tell him," Dessie answered.

"You mean, he doesn't know? Why? Is he married?

"No, "Dessie shook her head silently. "I wanted so badly to

have his baby, that I stopped thinking."

"Have you been to Father Solinka with this?"

"No. I needed to come to talk to you first. I don't know what to do," she answered.

"Well the first thing you must do, is get yourself to confession. You understand that there is no way I can resolve your sins. I can pray for you. And you know that I will. But only a priest can cleanse your soul by making what you have done right with God, Patricia." For the first time in all the years they had known each other, through school and beyond, the nun spoke Dessie's full Christian name, which she knew she had always hated to hear. It was as if she had slapped the girl in the face with her own punishment.

"And if you still believe you cannot talk to the boy, or the man responsible for this, then come and see me. Together we can work out a solution. You are not the first, Patricia," she said, aware how the girl winced at the use of her hated name. "But first you must go see Father Solinka."

***

Father Frank Solinka had grown weary with the Friday evening crowd lining up before his confessional. His absolutions had become rote, dealing with each infraction of God's laws with a weary assignment of contrite prayers. He was surprised to hear a voice from out of the past muttering from the penitent side of the confessional. "Bless me father, for I have sinned." It was a familiar voice, one he had not heard for some time. To be certain of what he heard and curious as to who it was, he moved closer to the screen separating the priest from the confessor to better see the penitent on the other side. Sure enough, through the mesh fabric, he could make out the silhouette of Desdemona Patricia Gonne. The priest hadn't seen the girl nor heard from her for several months. He cleared his throat and sat up.

"Yes, my child?"

And Dessie, made confident in the secrecy of the confessional, told him all, spelling out the details, including the name of the man who had made her pregnant and how she had lured him into making her pregnant.

"You are saying that you seduced the man?" the priest repeated with a note of incredulity.

"Yes I did Father," the girl answered.

"You do know that compounds your sin? And what is it that made you do this?"

"I don't know, Father. Except that I have wanted to have his baby from the moment I first saw him."

"I am assuming the man is not married?"

"He's not married, Father."

"I see," the priest replied, momentarily unsure of what to say, if anything.

"And what are the chances that one day you will marry him?"

"I am not going to marry him, Father."

"Is that because he is Jewish?"

"Oh no. I believed I loved him. This was the first time, Father. He is the only man with whom I have had those feelings of needing to have his baby."

"I see," the priest said softly. "And the man's name is Wolfe? That's not the family of the Wolfe & Bloomberg department store?" the priest asked.

"Yes, it is," Dessie whispered. It was getting progressively harder for her to utter the words of what it was she had done as the priest pressed her for details surrounding her sins.

"And what do you intend to do about this baby?" the priest asked.

"Sister Francis has told me she might have a plan," Dessie whispered.

"You went to see Sister Francis, before you came to

confession?"

"Yes Father."

"I see." The priest was about to explain the difference between confessing to a nun and confessing to a priest, knowing full well that the girl on the other side of the screen was aware of the difference. He decided it was best to skip the lecture and to avoid involving himself in whatever solution Sister Francis Clare was planning.

"I do absolve you from your sins, for I believe I detect a contrite and a confused soul. My heart goes out to you, as I am certain Jesus Christ's heart is reaching out to you. It is in the spirit of Jesus, who told the adulteress to go and sin no more, that I absolve you from your sins and admonish you to do the same. And Desdemona, whatever you do, do not compound the evil that you have already committed. You do understand what it is that I am saying?"

Dessie nodded.

"When you leave the confessional today, my child, you leave with a soul that has been cleansed of all evil, a soul made clean by the blood of our Lord and Savior Jesus Christ. For your penance, I want you to say a complete Rosary, with special emphasis on the Sorrowful Mysteries. Now go in peace," the priest said before launching into the Latin absolution.

CHAPTER 19: A CHILD IS BORN

It was difficult for Dessie to draw back from her relationship with Isaiah when she needed him more than she had ever thought possible. She wanted to reach out to him. He had come to look with anticipation to his visits to the Gonne house, basking in his newfound sense of himself, and became upset and petulant when she begged him to put off their love making. Yet he continued to try, only to learn the meaning of rejection, accompanied with Dessie's Irish cursing.

"For Christ sake, why can't you leave me alone?" she snapped at his repeated attempts to fondle her breasts. Having become accustomed to her yielding, his insecurity was quickly reborn.

Dessie stayed with her work schedule through the first seven months of her pregnancy, suffering the teasing, in-store jokes that implied her added weight was the result of too much of her sampling the candy inventory. It was a ruse she eventually encouraged.

At the suggestion of Sister Francis, Dessie met with the Salvation Army's White Shield home for pregnant, unwed girls. The Home agreed they would have a bed waiting for her, complete with the confidentiality that surrounded an unwanted pregnancy during the late thirties. Dessie applied for the time off from work and it was granted, ostensibly because of the coming summer season, though she never asked if a higher power had taken a hand.

The only question which she was unable to answer came during her pre-admission application to give birth in the Home. The uniformed Salvation Army Lieutenant asked her if she was prepared to discuss the adoption of her child. Dessie said no and accepted the White Shield offer to postpone her decision. The Lieutenant, confident that once she faced the stigma of being an unmarried mother, she would see the logic of giving the baby up for adoption.

Through all of the pre-birth preparations, Dessie's friendship with Isaiah withered and died with her refusing to continue their love making. Following his rejection – by the only friend he had known or trusted – he quickly reverted to the character that had won him tactical control of Wolfe & Bloomberg.

Dessie did however confess her pregnancy to her brother. She had to, and was pleased and believed him when he vowed never to speak of what she had done. Andrew also pressed her for a decision on what she intended to do with her child. She continued to refuse a commitment.

***

Dessie had never felt so completely alone as she did the morning she waited on the curb for the streetcar to carry her to the White Shield Home. Despite the early spring sunshine and the world around her blossoming with crocuses and daffodils, for her it was a uniquely painful feeling of being abandoned. In her mind and mood it was a more intense feeling of being alone than the morning in the rain when she had watched her father's casket being lowered into an open grave in the soldiers' cemetery.

There were other moments of intense abandonment in Dessie's life. She had spent weeks watching her mother slowly die as tuberculosis claimed her body. But even that could not compare with the devastation threatening to destroy her while she stood waiting in the morning sunshine for the streetcar.

She had been so young in those terrible days. As a child, she was able to remove herself from the feeling of abandonment; escaping as children so often do by denying the finality of death. Dessie believed she would one day meet her mother and the Sergeant Major in a happier life. That was what the church taught her to believe. She took refuge in the happier moments of mother and daughter, as if through a miracle those moments would live on. She was even able to shut out the voice of the drunken Seamus Ryan in the next room, raving that his Mary Louise was on the mend.

The difference? In the hard daylight of the early spring sunshine, Dessie was aware she was approaching the moment she would be separated from the life she felt growing within her for the past nine months; a child she talked to in the night, a child she had gently scolded when its movements shocked her. And the child in her womb spoke back to her in the mysterious language of mother and unborn babe. As for escaping to remembered happier times? That was a gift that was no longer available to this pregnant woman.

When the streetcar came into view, Dessie realized her thoughts were making her feelings of abandonment more intense.

She carried her small, cardboard suitcase. It was easy to carry, containing nothing but her toothbrush, a change of underwear and a new nightgown purchased at Wolfe & Bloomberg. There were thirteen dollars in her purse, which she planned to tuck into the toe of her shoe once she undressed in the Home. The rest of her money she left at home with Andrew to pay the household bills, trusting his commitment to resist reverting to his drinking.

It was midmorning, too late for the morning crowds on their way to work. Dessie chose a seat near the front of the empty car where the morning sun played warm on her face while she prayed silently for guidance, as well as for help and strength. And she longed to hold Isaiah's hand, even for a moment, recalling his touch, his hand in hers. If Isaiah were there with her, it would be different.

CHAPTER 20: THE WHITE SHIELD HOME

The Salvation Army's White Shield Home had once served as the West Hills mansion of an early timber baron. He gifted the house to the Salvation Army at his death. The building had since been painted white, as the stringent Salvation Army funding had allowed the house to settle into the neglect of decay. Once well-groomed lawns and gardens were now overgrown; the entrance hallway floors of inlaid mahogany and oak had been covered with runners of green linoleum for the convenience of easy cleaning. The intricate wood carvings of the stairwell bannisters and the built-in sideboard in the dining room were also painted white, perhaps reflecting the austerity Christians felt due the world's promiscuous women.

A heavy-set matron wearing a starched white nursing smock answered Dessie's doorbell ring, greeting her with a practiced welcoming smile. "You must be Desdemona Gonne. Sister Francis Clare has been calling about you. She has been asking me to let her know when you arrived."

"People call me Dessie," the girl at the door answered.

The nurse coughed, indicating she was unaccustomed to being interrupted. "We have a firm policy to never discuss patients over the telephone with anyone," she continued. "So I have told Sister Francis I could not say whether you had arrived or not. Perhaps you will explain that to her when you leave. Our visiting doctor will want to interview you later this afternoon. Why don't I show you to your bed where you can unpack your things for now. We can take care of the paperwork later," the matron continued without ever losing her smile.

The obstetrician who came to Dessie's room that afternoon was a Frenchman, with a heavy French accent. Dr. Rene Fulsher immediately informed her that he was vehemently opposed to any form of abortion under any and all circumstance. "That is why I come here to help young women to have their babies," he explained. "It is my reason for volunteering to deliver these babies at the White Shield Home."

"I'm Catholic," Dessie explained quietly.

"So am I," the doctor said, pleased to be dealing with someone of his own faith. "Perhaps I should confess, I am Catholic sometimes, eh?" He laughed.

"I have not had the opportunity to read the details of your religious beliefs. You will please excuse my not knowing everything I should? I like to explain my beliefs to all the girls who come here to find help," he said in his heavy French accent. "I will of course examine you. But you do look well, healthy enough for this, I mean," he laughed, a throaty, deep-chested laugh that sounded almost like a chest cough.

"There will be no problems, I promise you."

The doctor sat on the edge of her bed. "You should know that I was with the French Intelligence during the war. I am from Breton. That is my home. I was born there," he said hopefully, seeking some additional ties to this patient. "Breton. That is a province of France," he explained.

"Yes. I know," Dessie answered cautiously. "We learned that in our French classes."

"Parlez-vous François?" the doctor asked.

"Je parle un peu," Dessie replied haltingly. "I was never very good at languages. But my father served in France during the war and he spoke it better than I do, but not at all like the nuns taught us to speak."

"That is excellent," the doctor replied enthusiastically. "And how is your father these days?"

"He's dead. He died more than twenty years ago," Dessie replied.

"Aah, then we cannot speak French with him anymore, can

we," the doctor said. "The reason I am telling you all about myself, is because I have delivered many, many babies in France, and not always with the facilities we have at the White Shield Home, eh? In a barn? Yes. With cows and sheep, you see? Yes, of course. In fields, many times. In the desert too. In places you can only imagine. And God has blessed my work, because I have never lost a patient or a child." With that, the doctor smiled and crossed himself. "You are going to have a lovely baby. Now I will summon the nurse and we will examine you, yes?"

For the first time since she had awakened to the fact she was pregnant, and regarded herself lost beyond recall, Dessie smiled. "Thank you doctor," she said quietly. "Those are the first encouraging words I have heard in a very long time."

The doctor nodded wisely.

Three days later, with Dr. Fulsher attending, Dessie Gonne delivered her child, a six-pound four-ounce baby girl with ginger-colored hair and a traces of what would soon be bushy, wire-like eyebrows.

***

Dr. Fulsher, perhaps because he was French, perhaps because he had his practice in mind, did not conform to the unwritten White Shield Home rule of separating the newborn child from the birthing mother. Instead, he raised the bellowing new babe high in his hands, much like an athlete raising a trophy.

"You see. I told you. You have a beautiful daughter. Now what do you think of that?" he said, with that deep-chested laughter.

Dessie, exhausted from the several hours in labor, could only hold out her hands, reaching for the baby.

"Soon. Soon," the obstetrician promised. "Let the nurse clean her up, and then you shall hold your child. Is it not right?" he said turning to face the nursing attendant. "A mother who has worked so hard should hold her child, even for a brief moment or two. Yes?" he added rhetorically. "After all, it is the mother who has brought this baby into the world. She is entitled to hold her. No?"

The nurse shrugged, obviously unhappy that the mother was eagerly reaching for the child in the doctor's hands. "We have not yet made a decision on an adoption," she replied tersely, her lips barely moving as she spoke.

"Very well," the doctor said, settling the baby into Dessie's arms. "My work here is complete. Yes?

"Only now," he added, indicating Dessie, "it remains up to you to decide. If you choose to keep the child, you must remember that I am also a pediatrician?" He laughed again. "You know that in France, there are very many mothers with no husband. So you must think well, Desdemona," he said as the waiting nurse came over to the bed to claim the child.

The nurse frowned impatiently. "I believe we have said enough to confuse the girl, doctor. I suggest it's time to take the baby to the nursery while the mother rests. I will bring her back when she's ready to nurse."

"Oh, I know I can nurse her," Dessie said weakly, watching as the nurse left the room carrying her baby.

***

The second day after her delivery, following a brief discussion with Sister Francis Clare on the telephone, Dessie decided she would take the baby home to have her baptized by Father Solinka. Then she would think about adoption into a good Catholic family, or perhaps to Jewish parents, though she knew in her heart that was merely a passing thought, an obeisance to Isaiah. She still had a week of leave before she was due back at the store for the spring season sales.

The morning of her leaving the Home, she wrapped the baby in the shawl the Salvation White Shield Home provided to send out the adopted babies. She was saying her goodbyes to the two teenaged girls awaiting their delivery dates with Dr. Fulsher, when the matron who had greeted her at the front door came into the room.

"There is a gentleman in the front hall who claims he has come to drive you home today in his motor car. He didn't give me his name. He would say only that he is a friend. Would you like me to send him away?" the matron asked, convinced this was in fact the father.

"But I am not ready to see him," Dessie replied, assuming that Isaiah had discovered where she was. But then her thoughts quickly shifted to Sister Francis and she hesitated. "What if it is someone from the church?" she mused aloud. "Is there some way that I can see who it is?"

"You can look down into the front hall from the top of the stairs," the matron suggested.

Dessie, carrying the child in her arms, went to the railing at the top of the stairs. And there, looking up with a broad grin on his face, stood Patrick Higgins. "Hi," he called out. "You ready to go home?"

Higgins' motor car was an aging Moon convertible, a model the Moon Motor Car Company had long since ceased producing, as the company had gone out of business. Higgins tucked Dessie and her child into the two-seater, tossed her bag into the rumble seat and went around to the driver's side of the automobile, grinning all the while.

"Now," he announced, "if the old Moon will shine one more time?" He pushed down on the starter. The engine turned over, uncertain in its intent. Higgins inhaled and, holding his breath, tried the starter a second time. The motor coughed and sprang to life. "Ah ha," he hollered with glee. "Shine On Old Harvest Moon, for me and my gal, eh?"

"It's none of my business," he shouted over the clatter of the engine, "and I don't intend on making it any of my business. But you should think about including the father of the baby on this business. Regardless of whom he is, the man is entitled to know."

"No. This is something I have brought on myself," Dessie hollered over the rattling engine.

"Then listen to me. Have you ever heard of attorney client privilege?" Higgins continued to shout.

Dessie shook her head. "No."

"It is exactly like what we do in the confessional. Nobody, that is nobody, can divulge the things a client tells his attorney. If you feel so inclined, perhaps you could think more clearly about what lies ahead if you were to take advantage of attorney client privilege, and tell me what happened?" he hollered.

"First, I want to know how you happened to be here today," Dessie shouted back. "Who sent you?"

"Good question. When you get home, you will discover I had a call from Andrew. Your young brother called and asked to borrow the Moon so he could pick you up. I am still not too sure of that boy, or even aware that he knows how to drive. So I suggested I pick you up myself. No charge."

Dessie waited as the Moon rattled over the streetcar tracks and headed into the East End neighborhood before she spoke again. "He is really trying," she shouted. "Andrew, I mean. He is involved with AA. And yes, I need to talk to somebody, especially if I decide to put the baby up for adoption."

"If you decide? I thought that was a decision you had already made when you decided to bring the baby home," Higgins hollered. "They didn't appear very happy seeing you taking the baby from the White Shield Home."

Neither of them spoke again until Higgins parked the car in front of the Gonne family home and shut off the engine.

"I talked to Sister Francis, and if I go through with the adoption, it will be through the church," Dessie explained. "Before I tell you what happened, you should know that the only person I have told what happened is Father Frank Solinka," she said, adding quietly. "In the confessional."

For the following hour, sitting in the ancient Moon convertible outside the Gonne home while the baby slept in her arms, Dessie described how she had led Isaiah into seducing her. "I thought it must have been love," she explained. "But apparently it was simply my biological need, or a mystical calling. You can decide for yourself why it happened. But there was a need in me to have his baby. Maybe it was because of who he was; perhaps because he seemed so unobtainable? I don't know," she shrugged. "I only know that once I became pregnant, I couldn't do it anymore."

"It's your secret. Keep it as best you can," Higgins replied. "But I still believe you owe it to him to let him know."

***

There was never a doubt in Higgins' mind, nor in the mind of Dessie's brother Andrew, that she had already decided to keep the child. They both witnessed her fussing about the house the minute she arrived home with the baby. It was almost like a mother hen setting about nest building; only it was Dessie fussing to make room in her bedroom. When she finished, she turned to her brother, putting him to work.

"Andrew, you are the one who knows where to find things. We need a basket for your niece. See if you can find us a basket somewhere? And Andrew, be on the watch for a crib. The baby is going to need a place to sleep."

Down the block from Gonne house, a middle-aged woman had served as a wet nurse for a neighbor woman. Within the day of her arriving home, Dessie arranged for the woman's service. Two days later, convinced of the mothering instincts of the wet nurse, she negotiated an extension to the agreement to include a fee for day care.

The baptism took place three days later in front of the baptismal font of our Lady of Perpetual Help. In attendance were Higgins, Dessie Gonne, her bother Andrew and the inebriated Seamus Ryan, who had wandered in to the church in hopes there would be some form of a celebration to follow. Dessie chose the name Mary Louise in memory of the child's grandmother, and asked the priest to christen the baby with the name. That marked the end of any and all speculation over the possibility of adoption.

When her sick leave had passed, Dessie returned to clerking in the candy department in Wolfe & Bloomberg's main store. And while she occasionally saw Isaiah passing at a distance, he made it a point to walk out of his way so as not to pass near the candy and confections counter.

***

On a Saturday, four years following the birth of Dessie's child, her brother Andrew, with his niece Mary Louise trotting alongside to keep up, found himself without carfare home. He had taken Mary Louise to the Saturday matinée showing of the blockbuster movie 'Gone With The Wind'. Unable to deny the little girl anything she asked, he spent his last dime on popcorn and candy during the intermission. Though Dessie discouraged his dropping by the store, Andrew realized it was too long a walk for the little tyke. He could already feel her pulling on his hand, pleading with him to slow down. He decided he would slip into the store and borrow the carfare home from his sister.

It was now unusual for Isaiah to be in the store on Saturdays, but he was there that day, participating in the management surveillance program. He instigated the program himself, requiring the store managers to show up unexpectedly at any and all times in the company stores. It was a discipline he believed in and followed diligently himself.

At first glance, he failed to recognize Andrew, who was leading his niece by the hand. Yet something caused him to take a second glance.

"I know you. You are Andrew Gonne," Isaiah said, challenging Andrew to deny his identity.

"That's right," Andrew replied. He had already picked up the money from his sister and was headed out of the store. For a moment, he was at a loss to recall where it was he had seen this balding little man who was accosting him on the main floor of Wolfe & Bloomberg. "And you?" he asked, despite the fact he had suddenly remembered.

"Isaiah Wolfe. I run this store," the little man snapped. "And who is this? Your kid? I guess you got over all that drinking business, eh? What are you doing here? Shopping?"

Andrew was aware that Isaiah was recalling his indictment for lifting coins from the neighborhood milk bottles, and he guessed what was going through the little man's suspicious mind.

Isaiah was stalling him, waiting for the store detective, who in all probability had been watching this alcoholic shoplifting to feed his need for booze. Or maybe he had been to the candy counter and that sister of his had… Isaiah checked that thought, unwilling to entertain the suspicion out of a sense of loyalty to Dessie.

When the moment passed and it became obvious there was no detective on his trail, Andrew smiled and turned to leave, but not before Isaiah inextricably reached out to touch the ginger colored hair of the little girl reaching up for her uncle's hand.

"Congratulations. Nice kid," he mumbled and turned away.

***

There were other problems influencing Isaiah's withdrawing into himself besides his estrangement from Dessie. His mother's drinking had grown progressively worse so that there were days when she would collapse in the middle of lunch or dinner, sometime falling out of her chair to the floor or dropping her head onto the table in liquor-induced sleep. Alex Burns would then emerge from the kitchen, where he had been keeping an eye on her, and, with the help of staff, carry her up the sweeping staircase to her bed.

This situation reached a climactic moment when Rosa decided in the midst of a breakfast of tomato juice and vodka that she had unfinished business with Isaiah's boys' school in Bludenz. Grasping her walking stick, she rose unsteadily to her feet and called for Alex to bring the car around without her having packed a single bag.

The chauffeur had been instructed to call Isaiah at the store in the event of any display of erratic behavior. He called, and then, at Rosa's inebriated command, proceeded loading her into the new 1945 Packard, the car purchased by Isaiah for his mother. Once settled in the rear seat, Rosa reached out with her walking stick with an imperial tap on the chauffeur's shoulder. "To the airport, at once, dear Alex."

Fortunately for the chauffeur, he was saved from further embarrassment and confrontation as Isaiah's car appeared caroming into the driveway, followed by an ambulance with lights blazing, but no siren.

"I'll take over from here," Isaiah commanded, dismissing Alex. "I have already arranged for Mrs. Wolfe to be taken to a home where she can be looked after."

As he spoke, the ambulance attendants unloaded their stretcher and began preparing the straps to secure Rosa. "Mother, it will be just for a short while. You need someone to care for you for a few days," he assured his protesting mother.

"But I am leaving for Europe," Rosa wailed in her inebriated stupor as she was being lifted on to the stretcher. It passed unnoticed, but the aging Scot chauffeur made no attempt to conceal the tears running down his cheeks.

"Not today," Isaiah replied, signaling the attendants in the ambulance to take over.

"You can't do this. Who in hell do you think –" Rosa's parting words were cut off by the closing of the ambulance doors.

CHAPTER 21: A CALL FOR HELP

Slowly, with her wits returning with each passing day without alcohol, Rosa Wolfe began adjusting to her life in the home for Alzheimer's patients. It took several days of sobriety before she discovered she was a prisoner. All the perimeter doors were locked, with the staff carrying the keys needed to unlock the doors. And though Rosa could be wheeled into the gardens, and had her meals with others in the dining room, there was no chance of escaping the confines of the home.

In the weeks that followed, Isaiah was an infrequent visitor, and though he tried to dodge her confinement questions the few times that he did visit her, Rosa would continually bring the subject to his attention.

"You do know that I am a prisoner in this place," she demanded.

"You are not a prisoner," Isaiah argued. "You can come and go whenever you please."

"Then I will go home with you when you leave here today."

"That's not possible, mother. You have a contract with this care facility that states they will treat you until they are confident of your behavior when you leave." It was a lie and he knew it was a lie, but Isaiah had been lying to his mother since a child.

"Then why do I not have a telephone?"

"Who on earth would you want to call?" he asked, feigning modest surprise.

"I may want to call your father. If I do, I will tell him that you have me locked up in this place for people who have lost their minds."

"I'll see to it that there is a phone in your room when I leave," he promised wearily.

"You say that, like so many things you say you will do."

"It's a promise. You shall have a telephone and call whomever you choose," he said.

Isaiah was good to his word. When he left, he issued instructions his mother was to have a telephone in her room.

The following morning, Rosa watched silently when the man from the house service staff came to her room and plugged in her telephone. When he left, she went to the phone, picked up the receiver and waited for the dial tone. There was a pause and a click, and then the dial tone. She placed the receiver back in the cradle to think, now aware that her calls were to be monitored.

When her telephone rang early that afternoon, she answered the call. It was Isaiah.

"So, how's the phone working?" he asked cheerfully.

"It's fine," she answered.

"You call anyone yet?"

"No. But it's nice to have a call from you. What I need is a telephone book. Maybe I will want my hair dresser to stop by to touch up my grey hairs."

"You mean they didn't bring you a phone book? Let me see what I can do about that."

Within the hour the staff member returned with the phone book. Rosa thanked the man, leaving the book on the table until he left. When he was gone, she went to the book and looked up the name D.P. Gonne, transcribing the number on a slip of paper.

Rosa then watched the television in her room, a series of inane breakfast shows. She paid no attention, her mind was concentrated on other matters. When it came time for lunch she turned off the TV and left the room for the dining hall. On her arrival, she sat down at her assigned lunch table, and then quickly excusing herself, went to the desk by the door.

Addressing the staff person manning the desk, much like a head waiter stationed to remind patients of their proper seating places, she smiled. "You know they have installed a telephone in my room?" The woman at the desk returned her smile.

"That's great. Yes, I heard about that. That's a sign of a lot of improvement. Good for you," the desk manager replied.

"But I forgot to telephone my doctor. We are having tomatoe soup for dinner. I seem to remember his telling me that I was allergic to tomatoes. You think I could use your phone to call and check? I am really in the mood for tomatoe soup, and it sounds so very good."

"Certainly," the clerk said. "You go right ahead, and good luck." She handed Rosa the telephone off the desk.

Rosa dialed the Gonne number and when a male voice answered, she said: "Doctor Andrew. This is Rosa Wolfe. You remember me from General Hospital? I am calling from the Cedar Hills Resorts. That's a home for people with dementia, you understand."

The woman on the desk, overhearing the conversation, looked nervously surprised and shook her head negatively with a finger to her lips. "Don't say that," she mouthed. "This is not a home for dementia patients."

"Doctor, when you have a chance, could you drop in to see me? Tomorrow would be fine. I have some questions concerning the diet your office recommended about tomatoe soup. The home is on Skyline Drive. It is called Cedar Hills Resorts. Thank you, doctor." She handed the telephone back to the staff member. "He says I can have all the soup I want," she smiled.

The following morning, Dr. Andrew Gonne, a thirty-year-old who was impersonating a medical doctor, called at the Cedar Hills Resorts. Introducing himself as the family physician, he said he had been sent by Isaiah Wolfe to check up on Isaiah's mother, Rosa Wolfe. He was admitted, and for the next hour, talked privately with the patient in her room.

CHAPTER 22: THE STORE IS LOST

When Isaiah finished signing the documents invalidating his will and naming his new trustees, George Black and his lead litigator, Patrick Higgins, began gathering up the last of the records Lillian Zaronis had prepared for them.

"We will get back to you, first thing in the morning," Black promised. "Once Pat and I have had a chance to go through these records, we should be able to give you our thoughts on how to deal with your Bloomberg family problem. You are aware, of course, what your mother did in trading the real estate for stock appears to have created the problem. Your father knew what he was doing when he built those stores. What did he own? Seven separate real estate companies? Those properties were his ace in the hole in keeping the Bloomberg family shareholders at bay. There was no way they could oust Asa or you as long as you controlled those key sites."

"I figured that out the night she told me what she had done," Isaiah replied. "So what do we do about it?"

Isaiah had been calming down as the afternoon wore on, his confidence returning in the presence of the two attorneys. Yet what he said next startled George Black as the lawyers were about to leave.

"Higgins, I need you to you stick around for a minute. I want to discuss my new will."

"Isaiah, there is no new..." Black checked himself without finishing what he was about to say, suddenly aware that wasn't what the president and chairman of Wolfe & Bloomberg wanted to discuss.

Once they were alone, Isaiah got up from his chair and closed the office door. "Okay smart man," he began. "What's your story with Dessie Gonne? You know that I read the God damn play. How does it go? That line? 'Look to her, Moor, if thou hast eyes to see. She hath deceived her father and may thee.' I didn't get the message until after she dumped me. I assumed there was someone else. My guess is it was you."

Higgins shook his head knowingly. "Allow me to answer your guess, Mister Wolfe. I am a father with five kids in parochial school, plus one who is applying to Harvard Law School. That doesn't leave me much time to be involved or, for that matter, to even require a response to what I believe you are suggesting.

"Further, from what I know of Dessie Gonne, I would be surprised if she ever deceived anyone, especially you," Higgins replied. "There was another line in that play to which you have referred. It was spoken by Desdemona. She was sensing what lay ahead. 'And yet I fear you; for you are fatal then. Why I should fear I know not. Since guiltiness I know not; but yet I feel I fear."

"What are you trying to tell me?" Isaiah demanded.

Higgins, straight faced without a trace of guile, replied. "I once represented Miss Gonne's younger brother. That was a long time ago. He was a juvenile at the time and I have learned since that he too is attending school, studying pre-law. At the time I was engaged to represent him, the Juvenile Court was about to declare him a ward of the court."

"That's not what I want to know," Isaiah interrupted.

"As you can imagine, the boy has grown some since," Higgins continued. "I believe you ran into him the other day in your store. You may recall the young man with the little girl?"

Isaiah's face remained blank, though he had not forgotten that meeting, nor the little girl with the ginger-colored hair.

"That was Dessie Gonne's brother Andrew, as you apparently discovered. He had the impression you were questioning him because you suspected he was stealing from the store."

"And the child?" Isaiah asked, suddenly less sure of anything.

"Other than what I have revealed to you, Mister Wolfe, I am

bound by attorney-client confidentiality. And if you think that it pains me in not divulging additional details to you, then imagine how I am going to feel when I am forced to provide the same answer to my senior partner, George Black."

Isaiah sighed deeply. "Then I guess you might as well get t'hell outta here," Isaiah muttered, but in a manner and voice conveying to the lawyer that the little man was willing to accept Higgins' answer, and was perhaps even pleased.

***

George Black called back, not the first thing in the morning as he had promised, but late the following afternoon. "Isaiah, we have come up with troubling news. You told us that list of proxies you held was confidential. Well it seems it wasn't so confidential after all. Abe Rosenthal has called each and every one on the list for the express purpose of getting their pledge to vote for the sale.

"But that list..." Isaiah hesitated. "God damn her. There was no one who had that list but my secretary. I should have known. Zaronis called Rosenthal three or four times lately. I picked it up on the intercom. She was dialing on my extension. I knew it was Rosenthal's number."

"That explains things," Black replied. "Higgins and I have been canvassing each and every one of the Bloomberg cousins on that list of family members. We were concentrating on those whose proxies you have been voting. Each and every one we contacted has committed their shares to the sale of the company at thirty-eight dollars a share. It is a cash deal. We had difficulty understanding how Regal could afford to pay that kind of price based on company earnings. As it turned out, they couldn't.

"We have just gotten off the phone with our sources within the banking interests that are backing the sale. And while they have asked us to maintain the facts in strict confidence, I feel you are entitled to know the little that I am at liberty to reveal. It seems that Regal will be breaking the company into two pieces. Regal plans on continuing the publicly traded company reflecting the merchandising business sales and profits. You are familiar with those earnings. They have always been equitably reflected in the price of the Wolfe & Bloomberg common stock at eighteen to twenty-two dollars a share.

"However, Regal plans to spin off the real estate into a separate, privately held real estate company, into which they will transfer all of the Wolfe & Bloomberg real estate, including those seven real estate shopping center companies built and owned by your father, and exchanged for stock by your mother. Because he was against showing a large taxable income, Asa undervalued those properties, charging only depreciation and taxes in setting the rental rates to the trading company. You recall, his widow agreed to merge all his holdings at the then book value in exchange for company stock. Regal plans to hypothecate that real estate at valuations reflecting the true market value. That means the new leases will include a percentage of sales.

"Isaiah, that privately held real estate company is now worth at least five times the figure carried on the balance sheet. As we see the situation facing us, Regal has pledged the real estate at substantially increased valuations in securing the money they intend to borrow to purchase the firm.

"You may find it interesting that Regal has also made a deal with Jake Bloomberg, as well as one or two of the Bloomberg family executives, including your secretary, to make each of them minority partners in the real estate company. The irony is that the properties, once owned by your family, now belong, at least partially, to the Bloombergs. That gives Jacob and the others a share of the stepped up depreciation in the real estate which enables them, over time, to write off the substantial capital gains they will receive in the sale of the company.

"In addition, the Bloombergs and Zaronis will share in the

profits, if and when the real estate package is eventually sold. And our look at the history of Regal convinces us that's just a matter of time. Regal is not in the real estate holding business."

Through it all, mesmerized by Black's monotone recital, Isaiah stared with his eyes fixed on the eighth floor window of his office, seeing only the lingering impression of his lips and the rain dribbling down the glass. He was numbed listening to the facts he had long ago worked through his own mind.

"And Isaiah," Black added in a brief concluding blow, "I am afraid you were right in your assessment of Rosenthal. Abe took the basic idea of this deal to a half a dozen potential buyers once he convinced Rosa to swap the shopping centers for company stock. It merely required the boom in real estate values to bring Regal around to recognizing the values of the real estate.

"I am asking Pat Higgins to come over to your office in the morning with a complete breakdown of these figures for you to examine," Black added. "If, through some magic hat trick, you are able to come up with an offer better than the thirty-eight dollars a share, we could still upset their ballgame. There is always the possibility of another buyer. Our problem is that Regal has tied up the Bloomberg executives with the promise of cutting them in for a piece of the real estate company.

"Oh, and by the way, Isaiah. We have tentatively scheduled a meeting with your tax people for our office for Tuesday of next week. We are suggesting ten o'clock. Let us know if that meets with your schedule?"

Isaiah released the telephone from his hand letting it fall to the desk without uttering a word. His world was closing in, his nightmares had become realities.

CHAPTER 23: DESDEMONA'S RETURN

Out of habit that had become his every night routine, a routine that had been constantly practiced by his father – "You need to worry about every-day expenses, they add up over time and can lead to ruin. But don't concern yourself with one-time non-recurring expenditures. They can be handled." – Isaiah went about shutting off the office lights. He hit the main switch, leaving only the hallway light at the far end of the passage to the elevators. Then he stopped. There was a silhouette, someone was standing at the end of the hall, the figure outlined against the light. Instinct told him who it was, without his being able to see her face.

Dessie carried her coat over her arm. Even with the dim hall light at her back, he could see she wore her W & B black cotton dress, complete with the white lace collar recommended – in reality it was a requirement – for lady clerks. For a long, long moment, he didn't move, though he was as certain it was she.

"You had dinner?" Dessie Gonne asked softly in the quiet of the empty office corridor.

Isaiah felt his heart beating in his throat, accompanied by the uncomfortable pain in his chest that had been with him since the call from the attorneys. For a moment, he was undecided how to answer. So much time had passed. It must have been four or five years since they had lingered in his car and talked. Suddenly it came to him. She was all he had.

"No," he answered. "I'm not very hungry. How about a cup of tea? Or better still, I could use a stiff drink."

"You mean, it's that bad?" she suggested quietly.

"If it gets any worse…" he sighed, leaving the rest unspoken.

"Then I can tell you, it's no secret. At least not on the main floor. The gossip is all about the Bloomberg family selling the company."

Slowly, almost cautiously, the two began to approach one another, like wary cats on a mating prowl. When Dessie stood within reach, Isaiah could no longer help himself. She was an inch taller than he, and in her heels, he had to tilt his head slightly if he hoped to kiss her. He did, kissing her cheek.

"I don't know what you felt when I came up to you that day at the Ferris wheel," he said. "But when I told you my name, you said it was a name from the Bible and that I had been sent to you to remind you to study your Catechism. Sent by whom? An angel, you said. Who but an angel could send someone with a name like Isaiah?"

He stepped back, holding her at arm's length, as if to be sure she was really there in the dimly lit hallway. "Dessie, can't you see what I am beginning to believe? There is a destiny working in our lives. If I was sent to you for a reason, then there must be a reason that you are here tonight. You have been sent back to me for a reason. We Jews have angels too, you know. Lots of them. Perhaps you are one," he said smiling, and rising up onto the balls of his feet, he kissed her again.

And though there were dozens of gossiping clerks remaining on the main floor, Isaiah took her arm and for the first time, he and Dessie Gonne left the store arm in arm.

Not much was said in the car on the drive to the diner where they had spent so many evenings together. But once they were seated, Dessie with beer and Isaiah with hot water and whiskey, he unloaded the question that had been haunting him through the years. "Why did you dump me? What did I do that was so wrong?"

Dessie realized there was no reasonable explanation; no way for him to understand how she had wanted him to make her pregnant. Nor could she explain why. Just as there was no explanation he could be expected to accept, as to why she had never told him he had fathered her child.

Her first impulse was to turn the tables by demanding to know why it was Higgins, the lawyer sent by her brother, and not Isaiah who came to drive her home from the Salvation Army White Shield Home. Her first thought when the lady from the front door informed her there was a gentleman waiting to drive her home, she had been sure that it was Isaiah. He had missed her and discovered what she was going through. She had been prepared that day to explain everything. Until she went to the top of the stairs and discovered it was not the father of her child but the lawyer, looking up at her with a cheerful smile.

Instead, she began by asking him about his mother.

"What's my mother got to do with this?" Isaiah demanded, his brows drawn in a puzzled frown.

"You were her only child. There was nothing that could have taken you from her. And I was pregnant. I suspected you knew that, but didn't want to acknowledge the idea."

"You thought I couldn't handle it?" he asked, his voice reflecting a measure of indignation.

"I had planned to have your child. I seduced you. Is there no way that you can understand what your mother's reaction would be to that? Learning that you had knocked up, yes knocked up is the way it would be, an Irish Catholic girl? When I realized what I had done, and what I was facing, it was more than I could handle."

"The baby," Isaiah whispered, tugging at his shirt collar. "What happened to the baby?"

"You recall the little girl you ran into the other day when you stopped my brother in the store? That was our child. Andrew wasn't supposed to be in the store because of my asking him to stay away. He never told me he had met you. It was the child who told me. She said Uncle Andrew had been stopped by a man in the department store. When I asked her what man? It was as if she somehow knew. She described you, as only a four-year-old can, and then she told me that you had placed your hand on her head to touch her curls."

"I knew it," Isaiah's muttered, his words echoing the thought as it passed his mind. "It has been four years since...since we were together that way."

"Her name is Mary Louise. She was four last April."

"You should have told me," he mumbled, his thoughts passing inadvertently from his lips. "I need to see her again."

"Are you all right?" Dessie asked. She had noticed the sweat over his face and had been watching his incessant tugging at his collar as if he were unable to breathe.

He answered: "I'm okay. It's just that I want to see her."

Dessie decided to let it pass, attributing it to the hot whiskey or the excitement of the moment.

"It is past her bed time," she answered. "I can arrange for you to see her tomorrow, if that is what you want. It's good that you have the chance to think about it tonight. I don't want her to get her hopes running wild about meeting her daddy. Andrew is all the father she needs for tonight, at least. But we do have to talk about your mother. I have something to tell you."

"I told you, Rosa is in a place called Cedar Hills Resorts on the west side. It's for old people like her, most of who don't know or care what day it is. My mother had her car and driver half way out the driveway on her way to Austria or some damn place in Europe when I managed to cut her off. It's the booze. She can't handle it anymore."

"Andrew believes she can," Dessie replied.

"Andrew? Your brother? What the hell does he know about booze? Oh, I'm sorry. That's right. He spent ten days or so with my mother in the General Hospital clinic," he said, reverting to his sarcasm. "So now he is some kind of alcoholic expert?" Isaiah's voice was rising with indignation.

"Andrew hasn't touched alcohol since the day they sent him home. He has always maintained that when they sent Rosa home, she should have been allowed to stay for the extended treatment. He believes they wanted to get her out the door so they could get her into one of those expensive rehabilitation programs. One of the doctors at the General had an interest in a private alcoholic recovery place. He even suggested to Andrew that Andrew could use the additional programming. One look at the fees that went along with that suggestion and that idea flew out the window."

"So how did he do it? How did he stay sober?"

"He attended Alcoholics Anonymous, five and sometimes six or seven times a week for the better part of two years. And he credits your mother for the talks they had in the hospital alcoholic ward. He still attends meetings, now and then, because he thinks his success helps recovering alcoholics learn that they can succeed as well. Andrew has been sober for more than fourteen years."

Isaiah nodded with an acknowledging grunt. "He may be right. Mother did want to stay for the extended treatment. I thought it was because she was enjoying being with the young people, helping them with their recovery. I was against the idea of her staying in the program. I didn't want the world to know she has the drinking problem. I guess I should have called in a few outstanding favors."

"Andrew claims her helping someone else is the key to her staying off the bottle."

"At her age?" Isaiah asked doubtfully. "Rosa is in her sixties, though she won't admit it."

"He wants to try. He visited with her for an hour this afternoon."

"That's not possible. They don't allow strangers into the Cedar Hills Resorts. Those patients are all suffering with late-stage Alzheimer's. Most of them don't have the wits to be trusted in the outside world. That's why they keep them under lock and key."

"What Andrew asks is that you bring her home with you tomorrow morning about eleven. He suggests that you level with her that he is going to be there waiting for her when she arrives. And then step back and see if he has a handle on things, like he believes he does. The worst thing that can happen is that she belts a few and ends up back in Cedar Hills. "Andrew tells me your mother is pretty damn smart when she's not drinking."

"How did he get in to see her?"

"She telephoned him."

"They told me they were going to monitor her calls."

"Let me explain to you how smart she is," Dessie continued. "She called Andrew from the dining room desk telephone. She figured out on her own that her line was tapped. So she invented some excuse about calling her doctor from the dining room desk. Instead, she dialed Andrew and he showed up in answer to her call this morning, pretending and acting like Dr. Andrew whatever, saying he had been sent by you."

"I am about ready to try anything," Isaiah said, tugging at his shirt collar. "Tell your brother I will pick her up tomorrow morning about ten thirty and I should be at the estate by eleven. I will stop by Cedar Resorts tonight and tell her to get ready to leave."

"Look. It is obvious to me that you are not feeling well," Dessie said anxiously, watching him sweat. "You have been sitting there, tugging at your shirt collar and sweating so badly your shirt is soaked. And it's not that hot in here. I need to take you to the General Hospital and have the doctors look you over."

"You are right, as usual," he replied weakly. "I have got to do something with this God awful pain in my shoulder and my chest. It's been killing me since I hung up with the attorneys. There is no way I can be sick now. You picked up the rumors. The entire Bloomberg family is trying to pedal the company to a New York leverage buy-out firm. The only hope I have of saving the place is if I can somehow come up with another bidder. There is a major French retailer, Carrefour, that approached us last year. I sent them a telegram before I left the office. I know more about the true value of the company than..."

He paused as if to catch his breath. Dessie waited for him to finish, his face suddenly a death mask of ashen grey. She had seen her father turn that grey the morning he dropped dead at her feet during his inspection of her room. Isaiah had stopped speaking in mid-sentence, just as her father had in the midst of barking an order. She was reliving the Sergeant Major and his fatal attack when Isaiah's head fell to one side and he toppled over onto her lap.

By the time the ambulance turned into the General Hospital's emergency entrance, Isaiah had regained to consciousness and was attempting to force what he was saying through the oxygen mask the ambulance attendant held to his face. Dessie, seated alongside the gurney, held his hands. What he was saying was muffled and seemingly incomprehensible through the mask over his mouth and nose. But Dessie was sure she could make out the words.

"My God, please get me on my feet." Only Isaiah wasn't praying to God. Isaiah's plea was directed at Dessie.

A cardiologist was waiting for the ambulance in the emergency entrance, having been alerted by the driver. Without a second look, he barked an order at Dessie.

"You wait out here. He's having a heart attack, right now." Swiftly, the doctor reached for Isaiah's hand and began to trot alongside the gurney until they disappeared through the emergency operating room doors.

By two o'clock the following morning, the hospital, assuming she was family, offered Dessie an overnight room to lie down. Because it was near the Intensive Care unit where they had taken Isaiah, she accepted. The room, starkly naked with no windows, contained only a stiff-sheet, institutional single bed and one straight-back chair.

Without a thought, she turned off the light and was immediately in total darkness without a sense direction. She began groping along the walls in the dark until finally feeling her way to the bed. For the next several hours, she lay on her back, unsure whether her eyes were open or closed. Her thoughts reviewing a series of flashing pictures of all the possible scenes that may or may not occur.

In the morning when they knocked on her door, she called for them to come in, afraid to move from the bed in the pitch darkness of the room. It was only after the orderly opened the door that she was able to see and remember the nakedness of the room. The male orderly informed her that the doctor had given his permission for her to see Isaiah in the Intensive Care Unit, but only briefly.

It was a different Isaiah Wolfe from the man she knew. He looked even smaller in the full-sized bed, with his ghostly pale face and the intravenous tubes plugged into the backs of both hands. He managed to smile weakly and tried to shake his head and failed. "I should have moved you from candies to management. You have a way of always knowing what to do and when to do it," he said weakly.

"Don't try to talk," Dessie cautioned. "Just get well."

"The French Company," he began, and then smiled a painful smile, surrendering the idea. "What's the use?"

"Do you have any thoughts on how we go about getting your mother out of Cedar Hills Resorts?"

"If they ever give me a telephone," he began, before deciding to reveal what he had done. "Listen to me carefully. You are to call George Black. Black, Higgins, Kennedy, Gardner and…" he left the sentence unfinished. When he opened his eyes again, it appeared to pain him to speak.

"I have named you my living trustee. Black knows this and he knows who you are. Tell him to get her released..." He shut his eyes, too exhausted to go on. The Intensive Care nurse came up alongside the bed.

"He's had enough for now," the nurse whispered. "I believe you had better leave him to us."

Dessie went directly to the nursing station asking for a phone book and called the Black office from the hospital. When she asked to speak to George Black, she was put on hold. After a long pause, the switchboard operator came back on the line asking, "Can I tell Mister Black who is holding?"

"Tell him it's Desdemona Gonne."

"Desdemona? Like Shakespeare's Desdemona?" the operator asked, as if she hadn't heard correctly.

"Exactly," Dessie replied. George Black was on the line before she could finish her answer. In less time than it takes to retell, Dessie related the events of the past evening, including Isaiah's intention to free his mother from Cedar Hills Resorts.

"I can take care of that," Black answered. "Has he told you that you and I are his living trustees?"

"Yes, he has."

"Good. Now do you have somebody to pick Mrs. Wolfe up at the home? Or should I have someone call the Wolfe family driver?"

Dessie explained that Andrew Gonne would be at the resort before noon.

"One other thing," Black said. "Do you happen to recall the name of the French department store company where Isaiah sent the telegram?"

"It sounded like Carrefour, or something like that."

"Great. I know the company. They are a major French retailer. That may help. I will take it from there."

***

Andrew pulled up to the Cedar Hills Resorts at 10:55 a.m. He was driving Pat Higgins' Moon convertible, having bought the car from Higgins. He discovered Rosa Wolfe waiting impatiently in the lobby, a large suitcase and several packages stacked beside her chair.

All that Rosa had been told was that her son's attorneys had called relaying the word that Isaiah was unable to be there but that he had ordered her immediate discharge. The name of the law firm and George Black's personal call, following a brief call back to check the authenticity of the call, was enough for the Resorts to release their patient.

Seeing Andrew striding into the Resorts, Rosa leaned on her cane, struggling to her feet. “We did it,” she exclaimed. “I never thought you could pull it off.”

Andrew answered with a silent wink she immediately read as ‘say no more.’

“What happened to Alex, my driver?” Rosa demanded petulantly.

Andrew grinned. “Why? Won’t I do?”

“I guess you will have to, for now,” Rosa replied with an expression of faux skepticism. And for the first time since she had been admitted to Cedar Hills Resorts, the staff that had gathered to see their patient depart witnessed her smile.

Andrew had trouble loading all the luggage into the Moon rumble seat, most of which Rosa had ordered sent over following her arrival at the Resorts. Rosa had been a large woman when Asa first discovered her in the New York millinery warehouse, and the years had added substantial girth to her hips and bosom.

“Where are you taking me?” she asked adventurously, once Andrew had her settled in the snug seat of the coupe.

“I have a noon meeting to attend,” he said, glancing at his watch. “I had hoped you wouldn’t mind joining me. There may even be one or two of your old friends from the General Hospital there also.”

“AA?” Rosa suggested with a knowing look.

Andrew smiled. “We can stop and pick up lunch when the meeting is over. Then I have some things we need to discuss.”

***

The meeting was in the Unitarian Church lunchroom, a room used for church coffees on weekends. It was Rosa Wolfe’s first public Alcoholics Anonymous meeting and when it came time for her to speak, she stood among strangers – there were none of the young people she remembered from her hospital days – and said, somewhat shyly, for she was not a shy person by nature, "My name is Rosa Wolfe and I am an alcoholic."

That afternoon, over a drive-in lunch of burgers and soda, Andrew talked about his battle with alcohol; credited Rosa and the encouragement she had given him in the Hospital clinic as a source of his determination to stay sober.

When things became too tough to handle on his own, he told her how the AA twelve-step meetings had kept him in the program. And he admitted there were times when his craving for alcohol grew to be more than he could handle alone.

"Through all those bad times, I had a friend to call, a recovering alcoholic like I am. This friend would listen and understand what I was going through. If I needed him, he would get out of his bed to be with me for a while. My friend's favorite saying is always the same: Andrew. One drink is too many. A thousand drinks is not enough."

"If you like," he suggested to Rosa, "I would be that friend for you to call, any time, day or night. The only promise I make is to never scold you and to listen to what it is you are feeling. What I ask is that you think about what it is you are ready to handle. Okay?"

"I'll think about it," Rosa replied warily.

When he could see she was growing weary with his promises of progress, he asked her if she would like to meet a new friend.

"Anything that will get you off this subject," she laughed. "You are making me thirsty with all your talk about somebody or other having a drink. What about Isaiah," she asked. "Why wasn't my son there to see me sprung from that joint where he had me locked up?"

Andrew was forced to smile at her colloquialism.

"I learned to talk like that growing up in Brooklyn," Rosa

grinned.

"I had hoped we could get through the afternoon before we got to talking about your son," Andrew replied. "At least we did get through the meeting. What I have to tell you has come to me second-hand, so I only know what I have been told. Your son has had a heart attack and he is in the hospital Intensive Care Unit."

"I don't believe it," Rosa replied defiantly. "I know that boy. My God, here he is fifty years old and I am still calling him a boy. This is Isaiah's way of ducking out on this old lady having beaten him at his own game."

"I guess we all wish that were true," Andrew replied. "But my sister called and she's the one who told me your son is in the IC unit at the General Hospital."

"Your sister? What the hell has she got to do with this?"

"I am concerned I am unloading too much for you to handle at one time," Andrew said, waiting for her response.

"No. Give it to me straight. You are talking to a tough New York-born-bred woman. You really don't know much about me, do you, young man? There exists a side of me you know nothing about. So you damn well come clean or this friendship is in trouble, right now. What has your sister to do with this story you are telling me about my son?"

"Her name is Desdemona Patrician Gonne, though she hates to be called Patricia," Andrew began.

Rosa interrupted. "I know all that. I have known about her since she was a kid making eyes at my son."

"Do you also know that she is the mother of Isaiah's child?"

"A boy?" Rosa fired back.

"No. A girl. Her name is Mary Louise."

"Nice Christian name," Rosa said bitterly. "No wonder he has had a heart attack. How old is this baby?"

"She's four. She will be five in April"

"I knew this was going to happen from the moment he got off that damn Ferris wheel thirty years ago. The little fart told me he wasn't interested. I knew better. That's why I took him to Europe, to get her out of his system. I guess I should be grateful he's not gay. I thought for a long time he was."

"Look," Rosa sighed, "this old lady has had a tough day. Why don't you turn this piece of junk around and take me home."

"Because that's not the answer," Andrew said quietly. "You know why it is that you want to go there and what it will lead too. We are two blocks away from where your son's child lives. I want you to meet her before you make up your mind to do anything else."

"I'm not interested in cleaning up his mess," Rosa answered. "Just take me home."

***

The late Sergeant Major Gonne's dream home, purchased with a World War I soldier's mustering-out pay, was a two-story, stucco-finished house with a composition roof of tar-based green shingles. The front yard, once the Sergeant Major's pride, consisted of a fringe flower bed and what appeared to Rosa, from her view in the passenger seat of the Moon, as a weed-patch lawn. Andrew came around from the driver's side to open the passenger-side car door, recognizing Rosa's reluctance to get out of the car. He was also acknowledging her being accustomed to having her driver doing as much.

Seamus Ryan, the live-in ersatz husband of the late Mrs. Ryan (nee Gonne) had been gone since the day Dessie arrived home with her baby, having made his only appearance at the christening.

"Do we really have to do this?" Rosa sighed, reluctantly reaching for her cane.

Andrew merely smiled and nodded.

"Well then, let's get it over with," she added, though Andrew was sure he detected more than a hint of peaked curiosity as she approached the verandah. Rosa took the three steps to the front door, cautiously, one at a time, leaning on her cane at each step.

She had barely reached the first step when Mary Louise came bounding out the door to meet them on the verandah. The child had been dropped off at the Gonne house by her day-care neighbor from down the block on the strength of Andrew's promise to be home by three o'clock.

As a child, Mary Louise had pretty much grown up on her own. With Andrew attending his AA meetings in between classes at the Community College, and Dessie working full-time at Wolfe & Bloomberg. At the age of four and a half, she had taken it upon herself to learn how to load the dishwasher, fold down her bed in the morning and set the table for the evening supper. She had stationed herself at the window watching for the Moon in anticipation of Andrew's arrival and was out the door before Rosa and her uncle started up the steps.

"Rosa. Allow me to introduce Mary Louise," Andrew said with undisguised pride in the youngster. "Mary Louise, this is Mrs. Asa Wolfe. I believe I am not being too presumptuous by suggesting you may want to call her Mrs. Rosa Wolfe."

"Are you the lady who owns the store where Momma works?" the tyke asked innocently.

"Some people seem to think so," Rosa answered. "And I happen to know where you got all that red hair," she added, trying to sound stern.

"My Momma has hair colored like mine," the child answered.

Andrew held open the door into the living room, suggesting: "How about a cup of tea?"

Rosa heaved a second deep sigh as she dropped onto an overstuffed couch. "If that's all you have, I guess it will have to do. I had something a little stronger in mind."

Andrew laughed. "One day, one hour at a time," he said. "Surely we can handle that." As he disappeared into the kitchen, Rosa patted the cushion alongside her on the sofa. "Come and sit here next to me, Mary Louise, and tell me all about yourself."

"Well," the child began, wiggling up on the couch. "My mother says that I was born in the Salvation Army Hospital. I'm four and I will be five in April. Most of the time I am with Mrs. Kerr. She lives in a house down the block. Mrs. Kerr looks after me when Uncle Andrew is at school and my momma is working. Momma says I can start school early this fall. She thinks I can manage a year early, because I'm so smart."

"Why does that fail to surprise me," Rosa replied, relaxing with a whimsical smile. "And what is it you want to be when you grow up, to a young lady?"

Andrew brought in the tea as the child rattled off her dreams of becoming a fireman. "Or maybe a lawyer, like my Uncle Andrew wants to be. He has a good friend, Mister Higgins, who is helping him. Mister Higgins is a lawyer too. Or, sometimes I think I would like to be a nurse, so I could look after people like you when they get too old to look after themselves."

"You think I am too old to look after myself?" Rosa asked with a trace of indignation.

"Well, you need a walking stick to walk around."

"That's because I drink too much."

"Like my Uncle Andrew?"

"Used to," Andrew interjected, looking up from where he was pouring the tea.

"And what do you think about people who drink too much?" Rosa asked as the tyke wiggled further onto the couch.

"Andrew says they can't help it. He says it is a progressive illness. It is not something they want to do. He says it can never be cured, but it can be arrested." The child looked up at Andrew with a frown. "Is that like a policeman who has arrested someone?"

"Sort of," Andrew said. "It's kind of the same."

"That's right out of the AA handbook," Rosa laughed with a swift glance at Andrew.

"Mary Louise, how would you like to come home with me?"

Rosa said, her question startling Andrew. "I have a big house, much bigger than this house, and a yard you can play in. And there is a stable with one or two horses still there, I believe. We could get to know one another if you were to stay with me for a few days."

"But you said you drink too much," the child answered.

"Well, even the worst drunk can go a few days without taking a drink," Rosa said. "We will have to see if we can do something about that. Okay? Right now, this old lady is pretty tired," she added. "This has been a long day for me and I have a son who is in the hospital who needs me." She paused, before adding, "I think."

"Meanwhile, let's both you and me think about you coming to stay at my house awhile."

"Can I come and see your house now?" the little girl asked.

Andrew interrupted before Rosa could speak.

"Sweetheart, there is no room for you in the Moon," he said. "The car is filled with Rosa's luggage. I will take you to see her house some other time. Your mother should be home soon. Do you think you will be all right here alone in the house? Or should I walk you down the block to Mrs. Kerr?"

"No. I will be fine here. I have to set the table for dinner before Momma comes home," the child answered.

Rosa, struggling to her feet to leave, remarked quietly in an aside to Andrew, "If I believed in reincarnation, and I am not yet convinced it's all that it's cracked up to be, I would say that kid has been around for two or three lifetimes. She's what the rabbi once told me was an 'old soul'."

Mary Louise followed them to the verandah, waving goodbye as Andrew drove off, taking Rosa Wolfe home.

***

Rosa went that night without a drink, despite the fact Alex had left the bottle on the bedside table. The following morning, nerves and the confrontation visit she planned with Isaiah at the hospital, were too much. Before dressing she got up from bed, went to the cupboard where she had seen the glasses, returned to the bottle of vodka, and took a straight shot. Fortified, she picked up the telephone and called the General Hospital.

"I'm calling about my son, Isaiah Wolfe," she told the hospital operator. Told to wait one moment, she was switched to a nursing station and repeated what she had said to the first operator. This was followed by more of the same until she was finally connected to an intensive care nurse who confessed she had just come on duty.

"I am enquiring about my son, Isaiah Wolfe," Rosa said, her temper growing shorter by the minute. "I am told he is in your Intensive Care Unit because he suffered a heart attack. Is that true?" she demanded.

"Yes, he is here," the ICU nurse answered. "But you will have to talk to the doctors attending him for information concerning his condition."

"Can you at least tell me, is he alive, God dammit?" Rosa shouted into the phone.

"The doctor is not here this morning. However, I can give you his office number, if you would like. All I can tell you is that he is a patient," the nurse replied with an artificially calm voice. Rosa hung up the telephone and called Alex who was in the midst of having breakfast in his apartment over the garage.

"Alex, I need to have the car out front in twenty minutes. You know the way to the General Hospital? Good. That's where we are going. You can get your breakfast later." She dressed without fussing with her hair, slipped on a blonde wig, thought longingly about the bottle of vodka and one more for the road, and decided against it, hurrying out of her room before she could change her mind.

Having learned that Isaiah was in the hospital, Alex had the good sense not to press Rosa for answers she didn't have. Instead of his usual morning chatter, he drove the new Packard in total silence until he turned the car into the hospital driveway. Pulling up to the entrance, he quickly climbed out of the car. Alex, not as fast on his feet as he was as a younger man, discovered Rosa was already out of the car, cane in hand, hurrying toward the hospital entrance.

"I have no idea how long I am going to be," she called briskly over her shoulder as she passed through the lobby doors.

"Would you like me to park the car and..." Alex left the rest unsaid, realizing the lady was out of hearing.

Dessie Gonne had not left the hospital, having spent the entire night in the totally blacked-out, windowless sleeping room. She was sitting in the intensive care waiting room when Isaiah's mother came storming out of the elevator. Though Rosa had not seen Dessie for close to thirty years, she knew at once who it was. Perhaps to put the younger woman on the defensive, or maybe it was merely to be certain she was attacking the right person, she went directly up to Dessie, demanding. "And who are you?"

Despite the blonde wig, Dessie recognized the large woman with the cane as Isaiah's mother. "I'm Dessie," she answered.

"The Gonne woman. You are the Irish wench my son is supposed to have knocked up," Rosa said bitterly. "What are you doing here, anyway?"

"Waiting for you," Dessie replied quietly. "Now that you are here, I can go home knowing he is in the hands of someone who loves him."

"Wait a minute," Rosa said hurriedly. "I was rude, and I apologize. I am sorry. Don't leave, please. You and I have some things to discuss."

"There is really not much to discuss and very little anyone can do," Dessie added. "I was allowed to see him for a few minutes last night. If you let the nurses know who you are, they may let you in to see him. They have him pretty much sedated."

"Then you have been here all night?" Rosa asked.

"Since yesterday," Dessie replied.

"Was he... Were you two..." Rosa wanted to ask if they were fucking when Isaiah had the heart attack, but hesitated.

"We were having a drink together," Dessie said, anticipating the question. "He was upset with what is happening at the store. The lawyers called, and what they told him may have been the reason he is here."

"Let me find out if they will let me in to see him, and then we can go and get you some breakfast, or at least a coffee," Rosa said, attempting to sound civil. "I have some questions you can answer for me."

***

A somewhat subdued Rosa Wolfe was admitted into the ICU and permitted to stand by Isaiah's bed, though she was asked to put on a surgical face mask to protect the other patients. It took but one glance at the monitors rhythmically beeping over his bed and the tubes dripping into his arms to immediately alter the approach she had intended.

"How are you, son?" she said quietly. The words that had been on the tip of her tongue before coming up to the bedside had not been nearly so solicitous.

"This may be for the best, mother," Isaiah said quietly. "I am just sorry I have always been such a disappointment for you."

"The only time you ever disappointed me was when you grew up and were no longer my baby boy," she said. "Now you have that Desdemona Gonne out there in the hallway who has a baby girl she tells me is yours."

Isaiah managed to nod his head.

"Is it true?" Rosa asked. "Because I'm not sure if I want to be a grandmother to some little Irish-Jew. Just how sure are you?" Rosa said, some of the fire returning to her voice.

Isaiah merely nodded with a slight smile. “Is she still here?”

Rosa nodded, acknowledging she was. “In that case, we better be nice to her, because she’s still here. She tells me she’s been here all night. Was she the one who called the attorneys to get me out of that Cedar Hills Home for people who can’t remember their way home?” Rosa asked, beginning to connect the events of yesterday.

“Yes, she called them,” Isaiah answered.

“Mother, I don’t know if you have heard the news, but the Bloombergs have signed off on a deal to sell the company to a New York leverage buyout firm.”

“How can they do that when you control the stock?”

“It’s complicated, Mother, but they can. Let’s leave it at that.”

The old lady frowned and then, as if a light had gone on in her head, muttered. “The proxies, the Bloomberg proxies you voted? What happened?”

“The Bloomberg family exercised their votes in favor of the sale. I am not supposed to get upset thinking about these things. And if you want me to be around to one day get to see my child, we better drop the subject. That is what I meant when I suggested this may well be for the best.”

Rosa, who was very familiar with the business, didn’t need a map nor Isaiah’s spelling out the details as to where the fault lay. It left her momentarily speechless so that she was barely able to utter. “That bastard Rosenthal.”

“Mother,” Isaiah said quietly, “that wig does you no favors.”

***

It was a different Rosa Wolfe who emerged from the bedside meeting with her son. The first thing she did on leaving the unit was pull the blonde wig off her head and toss it onto an empty chair, then shake loose her dark yet greying hair. Dessie noticed the change, the physical deflation of the woman who had marched into the ICU prepared to deliver a piece of her mind. She decided to say nothing about the wig that had been cast aside.

Rosa appeared mentally confused, her mind remaining at Isaiah's bedside, so that it was Dessie who had to suggest, "Are you still interested in that coffee?"

"Yes. Oh yes, of course," Rosa answered and, with Dessie leading the way, they headed for the Hospital cafeteria.

Once settled over their coffee, Rosa confessed she had forgotten what it was she wanted to ask. However, she did go into her purse for a small medicine bottle with which she quickly, almost surreptitiously, spiked her coffee.

"You probably noticed the moment we met, before I went in to see Isaiah, I was somewhat hostile," Rosa began.

"Somewhat," Dessie agreed.

"I read once that we are not far removed from the monkeys that pee on the leaves in the jungle marking their territory. I remember the book. It was by someone named Tom or Thomas Ardsley. The book was The Territorial Imperative or something like that. I never realized how close to the mark that man's theory was until I recalled you and Isaiah climbing off that Ferris wheel. You, an Irish-bred Catholic, and Isaiah, my only child, a Jewish boy. I remembered seeing the way you looked at him that day. You were a threat to my territory, my son Isaiah. In that moment you became the encroaching monkey and you were pissing on my territorial leaves."

"I read that damn book…" Rosa mused. "Only now has it started to make sense, to my understanding why I attacked you like I did today."

"Do you think," Dessie said hesitatingly, "the book can explain why I did what I did in getting him into my bed? I have never been able to explain that in a way that made sense, even to the priest in confessional. I intend to read that book of yours, even though it sounds like something the church wouldn't encourage."

"What you did? That was just sex. You were horny," Rosa smiled dismissively. "I know something about being horny," she added with a sly grin. "I have lived most of my life with a reputation for being horny, which I always dismissed with a song I picked up from a Broadway show.

"If a customed tailored vet
Asks me out for something wet
When the vet begins to pet, I cry 'hooray.'
But I'm always true to you, Darlin', in my fashion
Yes, I'm always true to you, Darlin', in my way."

Rosa's attempt at supplying a tune to the lyrics broke the tension that had been almost visible since they first met, the two of them bursting into laughter.

"Andrew tells me you have met Mary Louise," Dessie said, wiping the laughter tears from her eyes.

"Yes. Yesterday," Rosa replied.

"And you invited her to come and stay with you awhile. Is that another chapter out of your book?"

"I suppose it is," Rosa answered. "I guess I was pissing on your leaves. Mary Louise may be your daughter, but the child is still my granddaughter. These territorial instincts make us do strange things."

"I think it would be good for her to stay with you for a while," Dessie said, surprising the older woman.

Rosa nodded in agreement. "When Isaiah comes home from the hospital, having someone around who wants to be a nurse someday may even help his recovery," she added, warming to the idea.

"She told you that, did she?" Dessie asked.

"Only that she wanted to look after old people like me who couldn't look after themselves. I didn't take that as much of a compliment, either."

There was a good feeling between the two when it came time to leave the hospital. Dessie asked the desk nurse for a telephone to call a cab, only to be interrupted by Rosa.

"Look. I have the car somewhere outside, if we can find my driver. Let me drive you home. It will be good for my aging and forgetful driver to know the way when he comes to pick up Mary Louise."

So they drove home together, the two of them in the back seat of the Packard, laughing and talking, mostly about Isaiah, though now and then Dessie would bring Mary Louise into the conversation.

CHAPTER 24: A VISIT FROM JACOB

Shortly after he was released from the intensive care unit and transferred to a private room in the hospital. Isaiah's nurse, following her instructions, came into his room to advise him he had a visitor. "Who is it?" he asked. Now that the word was out that he was in the hospital, he was not wanting to have a string of strangers dropping by to record their obeisance and putting him through a lot of idle chatter.

"The gentleman says his name is Jacob Bloomberg and he is somewhat insistent that you will want to see him."

Isaiah, aware that he was still the titular head of the company, was tempted to have cousin Jake come back another time. His better judgment prevailed. "Show him in," he said.

"Shit. You look half dead," were the first words out of Jake's mouth when he entered the room stinking of cigar smoke.

Jake had taken on many of the attributes of his father Nathan, weighing in at three hundred plus pounds. But where the elder Bloomberg had the height to carry off his being that heavy, young Jake never grew to the six feet three or four of his father. Thus all the three hundred pounds Jacob was carrying around were packed into a five-foot eight, stocky body which he attempted to disguise with tight fitting suits, merely accentuating his big belly.

"You don't look too good yourself," Isaiah replied.

"Never been better, which is a helluva lot more than you can say," Jake fired back. "Look, I didn't come here to waste my time swapping insults. You know we have the company sale locked up. It's a done deal. What the buyers are asking is that you come in on the sale with your stock. They are not happy with that much stock being voted against the deal."

"You have heard about my telegram to Carrefour, or you

wouldn't be here," Isaiah answered, absently tugging at his eyebrows with a smile. Isaiah had already heard in a call from George Black that the French merchant company was no longer interested in Wolfe & Bloomberg. The look on Jake's face told him Jake didn't know that.

"Look, good buddy," Jake grinned. "Let's get down to business. What will it take to get you on board? An office where you can come and go whenever you please? How about something to sweeten the pot, though thirty-six dollars a share is a very good price. But maybe we can do a little better for a large block like yours? Think about that."

Isaiah was sorry he had told the nurse to bring Jake into the room. There was some satisfaction when he mentioned Carrefour as that seemed to have upset Jake.

"If the offer of an office isn't enough, how about you staying on the board of directors for a year or so? You know we can arrange that as well. You are too damn smart to walk away from the business with a tip of your hat. The buyers seem to think the company needs you around," Jake blurted. "I think it's bullshit, but…" He left the rest unsaid.

"I will think about it and I'll talk to Rosa," Isaiah replied. "It's her stock."

"That's bullshit, and you know it," Jake said, his color rising. "Just don't get to thinking our willing to deal and to include you is open forever. The buyers want an answer soon. I'm outta here right now. But I'll be back tomorrow for your answer. Remember, the deal is done. We just don't want to leave you out in the cold."

"I'm touched," Isaiah muttered, the odor of stale cigar smoke lingering in the room long after Jake had left.

***

Once he was alone, Isaiah rang for his private nurse.

"I'm checking out of this place today," he told her. "I want you to call Alex, our family driver, and ask him to bring my clothes. Then call my doctor, tell him if he needs to see me, he can find me at home. He knows the way. Also call to let my mother know we are coming home. And here," he handed the nurse a slip of paper with a telephone number, "call that number and tell whoever answers that I want them all to meet me at my home this afternoon. Also, call my attorney George Black and tell him I will meet with him or Higgins at my home any time tomorrow.

"And nurse," he said in something of an afterthought as she busied herself making notes on her instructions. "I don't suppose you would consider giving up this nursing business for a job as my full-time secretary? At least think about it before you decide."

Isaiah was fully dressed when he stepped out of the ancient Packard that had been resurrected by Alex from the Wolfe garage to bring him home in style. It was immediately apparent to those in the welcoming committee that he had discarded his elevator shoes, looking even shorter than his five foot four. He wore a shirt open at the neck, a casual look for a middle-aged gentleman, and he appeared very frail. Alex was quick to offer his arm, ensuring Isaiah was able to stand. Isaiah quickly brushed him aside.

They were all there; a welcoming committee of Dessie Gonne, Rosa, Mary Louise and Andrew. Several of the house staff stood in the background, smiling, then joining the others when Dessie led the modest applause the moment Isaiah stepped out of the car.

During Isaiah's hospital stay, Rosa had installed an elevator to the second floor of the sprawling mansion and insisted on immediately leading him into the house to instruct him on the controls.

"I think we have both had enough of those sweeping stair treads," she explained. "Your father never liked them, in the first place."

"I happen to know a great deal about elevators," Isaiah smiled good naturedly. "My father spent more than a million dollars of the company money on those damn things. I shouldn't have too much trouble with this one. I'm just grateful you didn't get us into the home-style escalator business."

That afternoon at dinner, with Isaiah seated at the head of the table and eating almost nothing of what was put in front of him, Dessie startled them with an announcement. "I am not sure there will be much of a welcome awaiting me when I return to the store," she said. "So, if we can all agree with what I am considering is the right thing for Mary Louise, then I would like you to know that I am thinking of taking holy orders."

"Which means what, exactly?" Rosa demanded. She had been loud and aggressively exercising her role as the matron of the Wolfe estate all afternoon.

"It means I would become a teaching Sister."

"You mean a nun?" Rosa said with obvious skepticism.

"That's right. I have sent for introductions to several orders and eliminated some, those who were primarily looking for younger candidates. My thoughts now are somewhat in limbo, thought I feel I am suited for the Franciscan Montessori teaching order. It would mean I have to do some college work, but the order has indicated they are open to that. And I have always had regrets that I was never able to attend college. The question I need your advice and help with is deciding if I do this, whether I am being fair to Mary Louise."

"Where does that leave us?" Isaiah asked quietly from his place at the head of the table. As he spoke, he reached out to hold Mary Louise's hand atop the table. "I thought you and I had a future of some kind or the other."

"The whole thing sounds like a shitty idea to me," Rosa blurted. "What about her religion? Does she grow up an Irish Catholic or is there a bat mitzvah in her future?"

"That's something Mary Louise is going to have to decide, when the time comes," Isaiah answered quietly. "Whether she chooses a synagogue or a cathedral won't change my feelings.

She's my child, my only heir and yours as well, Mother," he said, addressing Rosa.

They were all aware that it was a tired and frail Isaiah who made that speech. Yet he took a long breath and went on.

"I have a meeting tomorrow with Jake Bloomberg," Isaiah continued, speaking softly. "Jake came to see me today in the hospital. He wants to have our family," he said looking at the opposite end of the table directly at Rosa, "as part of the sale. He offered several trivial benefits, but I suspect there is more to this than Jake was willing to let on."

"Just what do think he is really after?" Rosa asked.

"I don't think the buyers like the idea of Jacob running the company," Isaiah replied quietly.

"Well they certainly don't think you are going to do it, not while you are recovering from a near fatal heart attack," Rosa said. All the heads at the table were switching from one end of the table to the other, as if watching a tennis match.

"It was obvious to me that Jake did not know that Carrefour had notified George Black they were no longer interested in acquiring Wolfe & Bloomberg. So we will have to see how far he can be pushed," Isaiah sighed. "Meanwhile," he added, turning to Desdemona, "why don't you go on with your life as it is until we have all the answers. There may yet be a future for you and me. Right now, I'm dog tired and I need to rest before I fall over and make a scene. Dessie, do you think you could help put me to bed."

While his request directed to Dessie hurt Rosa, she said nothing, tossing her napkin to the table as if the dinner was finished.

It was Andrew, who had been listening to all this, who brought up the unfinished business of Rosa's drinking.

"My guess, Desdemona," he said, using a formal tone of voice, "is that you were counting on Isaiah being the new father in this family that you have somehow dreamed up for Mary Louise. I assume you envision Rosa as being her surrogate mother. We should all back off that idea, at least for now."

"What the hell are you getting at?" Rosa demanded, the tension at the table rising precipitously. "The child belongs here. Can't you see this is her home?"

"Everybody at this table, and that includes Mary Louise, recognizes that you are back on the bottle," Andrew answered quietly.

"So I take a drink now and then. In the past couple of weeks we have all been under a lot of stress with Isaiah coming home and the new elevator construction messing up the house. I think that I have proven that I can handle a drink now and then. It just takes a little will power. And Isaiah knows I have plenty of that."

"I didn't know you were drinking again," Isaiah said. "How much are you drinking?"

Andrew answered before Rosa could protest. "She is drinking every day, probably five or six times a day. I am partly to blame. I knew she wasn't ready when I brought her home to this place, knowing there was plenty of alcohol here. I was wrong leaving her alone."

"That's bullshit!" Rosa said, pushing her chair back from the table. "I have heard enough. I took one drink the morning I went to see my son in the hospital," she said, now glaring at Isaiah. "Since then, I believe I have proven that I can handle a drink now and then." She turned abruptly on her heels, staggered a moment without her cane and fell onto the floor.

Alex, who had been watching through the kitchen window, came out the kitchen doorway and went to her side, helping her to her feet. Rosa, accepting that her drinking had been exposed, grasped her cane, grinned sheepishly while leaning on Andrew's arm, and said upon leaving the room, "Thank God for that new elevator."

By late that afternoon, Rosa was laid out on her bed, passed out in a drunken sleep. Andrew volunteered to stay with her until she awoke, aware that her first move in attempting to solve her problem would be to take a drink.

Meanwhile, still at the table, Isaiah called Alex to task.

"I have concluded and now believe that you have been the go between in sustaining my mother's drinking, Alex. You don't need to explain. I know how persuasive she can be. However, I want you to pack up and move out of here, off the grounds by tomorrow morning. I suggest you visit my bank in the morning, see the manager, who will know you are coming, and he will explain your retirement income. It has all been taken care of."

"But I didn't have a choice," Alex protested. "You were in the hospital. And she would have fired me if I had come to you..."

Isaiah, demonstrating a flash of the character and management control that had won him the store, cut him off.

"That will be enough, Alex. You are endangering your pension with each word you speak to me from this moment on. I want you gone by morning."

With Andrew sitting with Rosa in her upstairs bedroom waiting until she awoke, and Mary Louise taken off to bed in the room that had been hers since she arrived at the Wolfe estate, there remained only a wearied Isaiah and Dessie left sitting at the long table.

"It is beginning to look as if you and I are going to have to assume the responsibility for our Mary Louise's future," Dessie smiled, staring thoughtfully at the wearied Isaiah. "I'm okay with my teaching dreams on hold if you really meant what you said about being a full-time father."

"Say no more," Isaiah said, turning to her with a slow smile. "You have a deal. And a good one, for you and our child, I promise. And now I'll ask you again. Dessie, do you think you could help me up to bed, with little or no promise of romancing me?" He attempted a mild chuckle but the effort failed him.

Isaiah died later that night with Desdemona Patricia Gonne holding his hands in hers.

As one of Isaiah's two trustees, Dessie was entitled to a percentage of his estate, an amount well over a million dollars.

Within a month, Rosa married her new driver, a younger man she introduced to Dessie and Mary Louise as Pierre. They were wed in a civil ceremony. Pierre remained her driver, and despite his hopes, he was never much more. She also succeeded in convincing Jacob to include her as a minority shareholder of the real estate properties, which were later sold.

Dessie grew wise in the business of administering Isaiah's estate and she remained in the Wolfe estate as a full-time mother until Mary Louise married at the age of eighteen, becoming the wife of a Jewish boy named Bloomberg. By then Dessie thought she was too old to go to college and past the years they were accepting women for holy orders. Instead, she opened a candy store in a poor neighborhood near the late Sergeant Major Gonne's former home and ended up giving most of her wares away to the neighborhood children.

Andrew went on to law school, graduating in four years, and joined Patrick Higgins in the firm of Black, Kendle and Higgins. He spent much of his time answering Rosa's calls for late-night counsel, and in representing people in trouble with alcohol.

The very first day of Jacob Bloomberg's assuming the management control of Wolfe & Bloomberg, Isaiah's name was painted from the curb in the company parking garage. At the same time, Asa's cubby-hole office on the sixth floor, the office Rosa had insisted was never to be touched, was turned into a storage locker for the maintenance crew. And a day or two later, when Pierre saw the company service truck enter the driveway of the Wolfe estate, he had been told what to expect. The driver had come for Isaiah's keys.

The driver was polite and apologetic. Wiping his hands on his company-issued coveralls, he held out his hand for the keys. Before he could speak, Pierre placed the keys into the palm of his hand. Then, with a wry grin, he reached out and took the driver's hand, the move startling the man. And they shook hands like departing friends.

True to George Black's prediction, the big store was sold again within two years to a national retailer and within a few more years following the original sale, the company was merged with still a larger retailer. Finally in one last blow to the heirs, the name Wolfe & Bloomberg was taken down from the marquee and disappeared from the company advertising. In its place there appeared a large neon sign and a new logo proclaiming the name of the surviving retail chain.

And the name Wolfe & Bloomberg? The merchandising giant that once had been referred to simply as 'The Big Store'? That survived, but only in the margins of memory of the very few who still showed up in hopes of a surprise.

THE END

www.ingramcontent.com/pod-product-compliance
Lightning Source LLC
LaVergne TN
LVHW090953080826
845145LV00003B/993

* 9 7 8 0 6 1 5 8 5 5 3 7 0 *